WYLDBLOOD

ISSUE 10 · AUTUMN 2022

IN THIS ISSUE:

Wyldblood Magazine #10, Autumn 2022. © 2022 Wyldblood Press and contributors.
ISBN-978-1-914417-11-5

Publisher: Wyldblood Press, Thicket View, Bakers Lane, Maidenhead SL6 6PX UK.
www.wyldblood.com **Editor:** Mark Bilsborough. **Fiction editor** Sandra Baker. **First readers:**
Vaughan Stanger, Mike Lewis, Rebecca Ruvinsky. **Subscriptions:** 6 issues epub/mobi/pdf
delivered to your inbox £18. 6 issue print subscriptions £30. Single issues available worldwide
via Amazon and from wyldblood.com/shop **Issue 11 will be published in January 2023**

Submissions: we are regularly open for submissions of flash fiction, short stories and novels –
check our website for our current status and requirements. We are a paying market. We also
need artwork, people to review us, and people to review *for* us. Email contact@wyldblood.com

Editorial

Mark Bilsborough

Welcome to the Autumn edition of *Wyldblood* – our last of the year, and our tenth issue. My rough maths tells me that's over 100 stories, not including the ones we've published every week on the website. We've had some good ones, too, and we're going to stick some of the best in an anthology which (fingers crossed) will be out before Christmas. We've also been wading through submissions for our *From the Depths* anthology, out in February, so we've been busy.

We've got twelve stories for you this time, ranging from hard SF to historic fantasy from Wyldblood regulars Mark Rigney, Lisa Short, Ephiny Gale and Rea Rees to Wyldblood newbies Alex Shvartsman, Renan Bernardo, Brandon Chinn. Emma Louise Gill, Paul Alex Gray, Connor Mellegers and Janna Miller. Fine stories abound, including some from our snap one-day submissions call for "After the Storm" stories (it was raining: we felt inspired and our Twitter page was coaxing us in...). Plus aliens, apocalypse(s) and the usual wistful stuff.

Ten issues feels like something we should mark in some way, so we'll be cracking open a bottle or two of Theakstone's Best (fine beer from Yorkshire) to celebrate in the Wyldbood offices and cheering on the *next* ten. But ten is list territory, and we love a good list (or five) so here are some of our 'best of' lists. We'll sprinkle a few more around the magazine where our writers have conveniently left us with gaps to fill.

These lists are all, of course, massively subjective so I'm sure everyone will disagree and hopefully you'll all send me an email to tell me *how much* you disagree and what you'd include instead (mark@wyldblood.com). And if you ask me tomorrow I'll come up with an entirely different list, and wonder why the hell I included most of the terrible novels I've listed this time. But if you're looking for good book recommendations, here's mine.

So: best science-fiction novels. #1 in my chart is **Iain M Banks' *The Player of Games***, one of his Culture novels set in the far future. I could have gone with any of the Culture novels so this one is a placeholder for the rest. Rich, thoughtful and inspiring. #2 is **Stephen King's *The Stand***, a compelling post-apocalyptic nightmare with a heavy hint of the supernatural (and it's arguably fantasy/horror, and at #3 I've gone for **M.R. Carey's *The Girl with All the Gifts***, despite my aversion to authors who use initials instead of proper names (I know we've published people who are shy about their first names in the past (and will continue to if the stories are great ones), but it doesn't mean I like it). Anyhow *The Girl with All the Gifts* is weirdly post-apocalyptical with credible zombies, which ticks loads of boxes for me. The rest of the sci-fi novel list is buried in the back pages.

Best fantasy novels are #1 *A Game of Thrones* by **George R.R Martin**, #2, **NK Jemsin's** *The Fifth Season* at #2 and **Jeanette NG's** *Under the Pendulum Sun*. *Game of Thrones* (and the rest *of Songs of Ice and Fire*) isn't particularly new, but it's very well written with impressive worldbuilding, sumptuous descriptions and well-drawn and engaging characters. Likewise *Fifth Season* and *Pendulum Sun* – competent fantasy (and steampunk) from impressive new (ish) writers. Full list later.

All our other lists are TV and film. Best SF *Aliens* (film) and *Battlestar Galactica* (the remake, obs) (TV). Best Fantasy: *Lord of the Rings: The Fellowship of the Rings* (film) and *Shadow and Bone* (TV.; Best Superhero: *The Umbrella Academy* (TV) and *Spider Man – No Way Home* (film). Best Dr Who; David Tennant. Best Star Trek captain: Kirk (best series *Strange New Worlds*). I could do this all day, but you've got stories to read and I need to *focus.*

So have I got it right or is my taste so egregious that you need to write immediately to correct me and offer more stirring suggestions? Either way, get in touch.

Lastly, if any of you are looking for an online critiquing group the BSFA (British Science Fiction Association) has a few: they split into groups for novels and groups for short stories (though you can be in both) – five people in each, roughly a short story or novel extract to the group every two months in return for nice, friendly constructive feedback and they're free to BSFA members (rates vary between cheap and cheapish but you don't have to be British to join, and these groups are online). The BSFA is at www.bsfa.co.uk

Enjoy the stories,

Mark

Love in the Apocalypse

A Little Longer

M. A. Dosser

"What will it be like?" Nelia asked.

"Which part?" Kayla replied, her voice nearly lost under the approaching bomb's metallic screech.

From up on their hilltop, they could see people fleeing in droves. The evacuation siren had been blaring for thirty minutes. Not nearly enough time.

"It should be quick," Kayla said.

"Hopefully. But this moment can last a little longer," Nelia rested her head on Kayla's shoulder. They smiled at each other—eyes for no one or nothing else.

Not even the fireball on impact. Or the house obliterated by the shockwave. Or the debris flying in their direction.

M.A. Dosser is a PhD candidate at the University of Pittsburgh. He is the co-founder and editor of Flash Point SF and his own fiction has recently appeared or is forthcoming in publications such as Daily Science Fiction, Land Beyond the World, and Martian: The Magazine of Science Fiction Drabbles.

A Cup of Empathy

Ria Rees

"Plain Gratitude, no whip." The patron glares through his bushy eyebrows.

My eyes flick automatically to their bracelet—black stripe, one dash. I bow in respect and tap the order screen between us. "Would you care for an extra shot of Empathy, sir?"

"No."

Well yeah, that tracks. It's a shame, too—we had a fresh batch of Empathy today. I enjoyed a small cup earlier—my only employee perk. Frank subs us a free daily drink, so long as it improves our performance, but they're usually the cheaper varieties. I like Empathy; it helps me get a feel for the client's mood. Sometimes I'll take a shot of Vigilance if it's been a really rough night.

Prep comes easily; I've worked at Emotive for five years—I may as well be an automaton.

First, I swill the water around to air out the chemical scent of the purifiers. Then I pour it into a small glass with an artful flourish, followed by a single shot of ice-blue Gratitude. The patron taps their bracelet against the bar, and the till beeps to confirm payment. I slide the glass over the counter. Just like an industrial factory.

"Thank you, Sir." I beam in plastic. Mr Gratitude needs to see someone smile at him today, even if it's just for show.

He grabs the shot and downs it, and his face immediately morphs: The jaw slackens, the eyes crinkle at the corners, and a beaming grin lights up his face. "No, no, dear, thank *you*. Isn't it a beautiful evening?"

"Just the best." I smile as he saunters out into the neon streets, goggling at the satellites streaming through the night sky. He pauses at every marketing screen, waving at the giant, too-perfect faces grinning from above.

Most patrons come by every day, same time, same order. I try to imagine their stories in my downtime. Sometimes I even ask them when I'm feeling courageous.

I wonder what Gratitude's life is like as a VIP. It felt like he had a rough day–perhaps

4

he had to demote a worker. Or worse, maybe he had to abandon someone. I imagine it must be hard to feel thankful when your job entails stamping on someone's face like that.

"The system needs flushing, Connie, while there's a gap," Frank calls from the back room.

I attend to the pumps on the back wall, cleaning the tubes and flushing the older syrups through the system. The syrup barrels are all stored in the basement. I wonder how many months I'd have to work to cover the cost of a single cask.

"Excuse me, young miss?" A shaky voice says behind me.

I turn around to find an old patron hunched over the counter. Their tattered clothes are barely covered by a plastic raincoat, the kind you fold and pack in your pocket. It crinkles with every movement.

I automatically check his wrists. No bracelet. He's Abandoned.

"Oh, hello…" I stammer, my hands tremble.

Five years and this has never happened to me — This. Never. Happens. Abandoned don't come in here; they know the rules. They keep to the dark alleys and underground of the city — so long as they keep out of the Warden's way, they're left alone.

"You can call me John, thank you."

He thinks I'm going to serve him. He can't. He must know how this works? But oh, he's still talking…

"Young miss, could I trouble you for a cup of water?" He holds a steel camping cup, hands trembling from the effort. "It's so hot tonight, and the drains are dry."

My stomach flips. Do Abandoned drink from the storm drains? I've never put myself in their position before. It's never even occurred to me to try. The thought brings a lump into my throat, but it's curfew soon, and Wardens are bound to notice an Abandoned trooping around the streets.

"Erm. I'm sorry, I'm not sure I can—" I point to a sign behind the counter; No bracelet, no earnings, no service.

John's face falls, but he nods. "Yes, yes, of course. I knew that of course, but—never mind. Thank you…?" He raises his eyebrows in that old fashioned way, to ask my name.

"Connie," I say, though I can't keep my eyes on him — I'm too paranoid that someone will see us, so I keep checking the streets. It's busy outside, but nobody seems to be paying us any attention, and there aren't any Wardens on duty yet.

The Empathy rushing through my bloodstream tuts and judges me. *You're better than this, Connie.*

My gaze falls on Frank, who's now leaning back in his chair, peering out from the back room with a frown. He sees John and shakes his head at me, waving his hand dismissively. There's panic in his eyes. I nod and turn back to John. "I'm really sorry."

"I understand, dear." He smiles, the wrinkles in his face creasing further, and leaves.

He shuffles out of sight just as the buzzer sounds, and a new patron arrives. They gaze at the menu board, oblivious to my presence. I take a deep breath to centre myself and glance at their bracelet — white stripe, two-dash. Non-Binary worker. They work at the automata factory by the looks of their greasy hands. Studying their face, it feels like they work better with machines than with people.

"Uh… half-carb Mondo… Soy… Focus…" They trail off, apparently finished, but I wait another moment — there's more.

They raise a finger, "—with an extra shot."

I nod and begin steaming the milk. "Whip?" I shout over the din.

"Sorry? Erm… No, no whip."

The soy milk froths up to the top of the jug, I pour three-quarters of it into a large mug. Two shots of half-carb Focus, tilt the mug and wiggle the foam on top, just so. It's beautiful, a work of art, really. But John's sad eyes are looking up at me from the pattern in the foam, shaking his head as the liquid settles.

Come on, snap out of it, Connie.

Serve, smile, simper. "Thank you, Mix."

"Mmm." They start to wander off.

"Erm, Mix? Your payment?"

"Oh, of course." They turn back and tap the counter with their wrist. I imagine it'll take at least half the mug before they even remember what project they were working on.

Jerry glides in, wearing his own plastic smile, but now even his eyes look like John's to me.

"Hey, Connie. Same as usual, with an extra shot today, please?"

Large mug, steaming hot oat milk, two shots of Fulfilment. I stare at the surface, transfixed as the purple-mauve syrup mingles and combines with the milk.

I hide behind machinery and inhale the steam. I always do this with Jerry's order, hoping to absorb even a hint of the satisfaction he's about to consume. I remind myself that Fulfilment never used to come in barrels. How did anyone get by–what could they possibly have back then that made them feel this way? I inhale deeply, and a warm tingle rushes down my neck.

Frank coughs from his desk out back. I'm taking too long, again.

"Sorry, Frank, on it!" I hastily click the top and hand it across the counter with a smile. "Thank you, Sir."

"Jerry!" He corrects me with a grin.

I smile, silent. No, it's always Sir (black stripe), Madam (blue stripe), Mix (white stripe). Check the bracelet first, honorifics and earnings. One dash for VIPs, two dashes for workers.

And the rest… well… No bracelet.

No bracelet, no earnings, no service.

That never came up, until tonight.

Jerry leaves, guzzling his Fulfilment with gusto.

"I'll take a zero-carb mondo Serenity with a shot of Oblivion, no whip." Blue stripe, one dash. Tailored suit and high heels, impeccable makeup, tight, sleek bun.

"No whip, Madam?" I'm genuinely stunned, "but… it's Serenity?"

She nods curtly. "I'm on a diet."

"Oh, uh…" Dammit—I should have picked up on that. I stammer and fumble around behind the counter as the patron rolls her eyes. "I'm afraid we don't have Serenity in zero-carb, madam."

"Why not?"

"Well, uh…" I look helplessly at Frank, who walks out with his chest puffed.

"Can I help you, madam?" He laces his fingers together, immediately adopting the air of the negotiator.

She taps a too-long fingernail on the counter. "Your girl here, she says you don't have zero-carb Serenity! Preposterous!"

Frank nods sagely. "Indeed, madam. A shortcoming on our part, of course."

The customer is always right. But, if they're a VIP, they're not just right; they're infallible.

"Perhaps we could give you a free sample by way of apology?" He beckons to me behind his back, and I sneak him a half-shot of Understanding, grinning at the patron.

"This is the latest beverage from Emotive! Give it a try, on the house."

She sniffs it uncertainly.

"Please don't worry. It's low-carb and quite delicious."

A single sip and her face relaxes. "Oh, that's new. You know what, I think the standard Serenity will do just fine. What's one drink, after all?"

"Excellent, madam."

Frank and I share a conspiratorial look as I prepare her giant drink, glad we've succeeded this time. The last time a VIP started getting angry in the cafe, they called Wardens in. Negotiating with them is much more difficult than just dosing them up.

We'd both be abandoned in a heartbeat if we even tried it.

The sunset orange Serenity mingles with the black half-shot of Oblivion. I never use a full shot. That's a Warden's prerogative. But a half shot is more than enough to get the desired effect. Not catatonic, just… nicely blissed out.

The night wears on, and the queues dwindle. I start putting supplies away and tidying up behind the counter ready to lock up. I get down on the floor to clean the back of the lower shelves under the counter and lose myself in another menial task.

"Excuse me, young miss?"

I peek over the counter and see John. Twice in one day–I realise he must be losing his memory. He doesn't seem to remember coming in just a few hours ago. He stands at the counter with his innocent, wrinkled smile, waiting patiently for me to serve him. Does he remember his old life? Maybe he's reliving those days.

I need to tell him to leave, but I picture myself leaning over the storm drains outside, reaching shoulder-deep for water. I curl up on a street corner, sharing the concrete with rats and cardboard, and shiver under the all-seeing satellites, ignored by workers, spat on by VIPs. I run from Wardens and find more of my kind, but my belly rumbles, and my tongue is sand in my mouth.

My heart aches.

"I wonder, miss, if you could…" He holds out his cup.

We're alone in the cafe; I check in every darkened corner. Frank laughs on the phone in the office, totally unaware of John's presence. He's dropped his guard now that the patrons are gone.

Only three minutes till closing time. Wardens will come soon on a curfew sweep. If they see John, we'll both be taken.

My sweet, fresh cup of Empathy tugs my heartstrings. It moves my arms like I'm a marionette, betraying all common sense. Breaking the rules.

"Here." I watch my arm reach across the counter and grab his cup, filling it with water from the tank. My jaw drops as my hands shove the mug under the Luck spout and pump in a shot. In a mechanical motion I've performed hundreds of times a day, I swirl the cup, mixing the yellow syrup with the chemically purified water.

I hold the cup out to John and sense sudden movement in my peripheral vision—Frank has finished on the phone.

John drinks greedily, lapping at the water like a puppy. "Thank you so much, Miss. What is your name?"

"Connie", I whisper hurriedly. "I'm sorry, but you need to go. You can't let them find you."

I dart round the counter and usher John outside. He staggers into the road, narrowly avoiding collision with four cars before finding his feet. He turns and waves at me from the middle of the street—three more cars beep their horns and swerve to avoid him. He disappears down an alley, and I dash back inside.

"What did you do?" Frank is frozen at his office door. White-faced, jaw slack, sweat beading on his forehead. "Connie, what the fuck did you do?"

I close the door, flip the lights off, and rush over. "Frank, please, I didn't do anything. I just sent him on his way—"

"Liar." He points at me, his arm shaking. "I saw you hand it to him. I already set off the alarm. Wardens will be here soon. I…" the anger on his face melts, giving way to fear. "I'm sorry, Connie."

My heart pounds in my chest. I want to scream at him—how dare you! I trusted you! But I understand; he had no choice. He knows the rules.

Frank runs through the back exit. It bangs against the outside alley wall. I stand alone in the darkened cafe as the curfew siren wails through the streets.

Time's running out. I vault over the counter and reach the pump labelled 'Luck'.

One squirt into my open palm is all I need. My cupped hand reaches my chin when the door smashes open behind me.

"Hands up!"

Frozen on the spot, a single shot of Luck dribbling between my fingers and down to my elbow. My hands reach the ceiling, and the Warden binds my wrists.

"What were you thinking? You know the rules." He's firm, strict, but his voice has a softness. It doesn't matter, though. He won't go easy on me.

"I don't know; this never happens." Tears stream down my cheeks. Everything hurts—the pain, the betrayal of my own body, John's sad eyes, Jerry's plastic smile, Gratitude and Focus and Serenity… The Warden's cold certainty, their black-and-white brain ticking through procedure. "It was the Empathy… I'm sorry—"

He yanks me by the arm, dragging me to a chair, and pushes me down. "No time for that. Open up."

"Oh no, please—"

His partner approaches me with a bottle filled with black Oblivion—a much stronger distillation than we sell, only legal for Wardens to carry. I clamp my lips shut and wiggle on the chair, desperate to keep my sanity.

The Warden holds my chin, forces my mouth open and tilts my head back, pouring the liquid Oblivion down my throat. They pinch my nose and force me to swallow. I'm vaguely aware of my bracelet being cut before they push me out alone on the streets. Abandoned.

"Blue stripe, two dash…" I chuckle.

The voice doesn't belong to Connie anymore, not once the Oblivion begins to pulse through her veins.

Who's Connie?

We slide down the wall and sit with our arms limp on the road.

The street noises fade to distant buzzing.

We tilt our heads and goggle at the satellites streaking across the sky.

We're so thirsty.

Ria Rees *writes from her cosy cottage in Wales, praying that her creations will never become sentient. Her first loves in fiction were Horror and Sci-Fi, and she leaps at any chance she gets to combine the two. Her work is published or forthcoming in Fantasy & Science Fiction Magazine, Bag of Bones Press and Wyldblood Magazine.* *www.riarees.com*

The Wyldblood 10th issue
10 Best lists

10 best science fiction films

Aliens/Alien
The Matrix
Blade Runner
Serenity
Prey
Rogue One
Terminator
Edge of Tomorrow
The Fifth Element
Star Trek: First Contact

In This Last of Meeting Places

Lisa Short

Lightning struck outside the cabin again and again. Each time it hit, the air inside was flooded with brilliance, blinding Mia with writhing white afterimages and then deafening her with thunder that shook the cabin walls even more than the wind did. Sherry and the coydog pup stayed hidden under a blanket on the floor, only peeking out occasionally to make sure Mia hadn't gone anywhere. Mia's emotional reserves were mostly exhausted, but she did feel a faint spark of humor in the periodic appearance of those two sets of anxious eyes, blue and brown, peering out at her from the blanket's folds. Only a seven-year-old or a puppy would think there was anywhere for her to go.

She wasn't sure how long the three of them remained crouched there, up against the wall farthest from the cabin's only window. Eventually, though, the lightning faded away and the rain gentled into a soft, steady patter against the cabin roof. Mia had nearly fallen asleep when a rustling, scratching noise startled her awake. Sherry was emerging from the blanket, the pup clutched in her arms, his long hind legs scrabbling against the battered wood floor.

"He's trying to get away," Sherry said. Her eyes were round and solemn over the top of the pup's tossing head.

"He probably has to pee."

"I don't want to let him outside, Mia! What if the storm starts again?"

"It won't," said Mia bracingly, though she didn't have the faintest idea if it would or not.

"You promise?"

"I promise."

Sherry staggered across the cabin, swerving around the puddles that had bloomed on the floor near the window. Once she got the door wedged a few inches open, the pup squeezed his stocky little frame through the gap and vanished outside. Sherry turned back to look at Mia, her bottom lip trembling. "He will come back, won't he?"

"Hasn't he always?" Not to Mia's delight—their parents hadn't thought to store any dog food in the cabin. The pup had to share what she and Sherry ate, and he ate a lot.

But Sherry was comforted and trotted back to Mia's side, dropping down on the floor to snuggle up against her shoulder. Mia craned her neck sideways to give the top of her sister's sticky, matted curls a kiss; she supposed she would have to figure out a way to bathe all three of them at some point. There was a crate next to the woodpile stacked up against the cabin wall with SUNDRIES scrawled across its side, which probably included soap—but every time she thought of it, or of doing anything else not absolutely required to keep Sherry immediately alive and safe, she was swamped by a wave of black indifference.

"Mia?"

"Hmm?"

"When are Mommy and Daddy coming?"

"Soon," said Mia.

"But how soon?"

"I don't know. Their note didn't say, remember?"

"So how do you *know* it's soon?"

They'd had this conversation before. "Sherry—"

"Don't get mad," said Sherry unhappily. She paused. "Can you read the note to me again?"

Mia stifled a sigh, then lifted her bottom up off the ground long enough to wiggle the folded paper out of her back pocket. After she settled back down against the cabin wall, Sherry climbed onto her lap and wrapped her arms tightly around her sister. Mia lifted the scrap of paper up to the dim gray light seeping through the shutters and squinted at it, though she'd long since memorized its contents. "'Take your sister to the cabin, there's enough food and fuel stocked there to get you through the winter,'" she recited. "'The guns—'"

"*Mia,*" Sherry moaned. "What if there isn't enough food and stuff to get *all* of us through the winter, with Mommy and Daddy *and* Coy?"

"Is that what you've decided to name the pup? Coy?"

"Yeah. Coy. Because he's a coypup, you said so when we found him. Is there enough food for all of us?"

"Yes," said Mia. "Do you want me to finish reading or not?"

Sherry nodded violently.

"Okay. 'The guns are locked in the shed, along with some other gear that should help you girls out,'" she finished, and started to refold the note. Sherry let go of her long enough to stretch out a hand towards it. "What, honey?"

"Can I hold it?"

"Sure. Just be careful, okay?"

"I will." Sherry's tight grip crumpled the note's edges, but it didn't really matter. "Take…your…sister…to…the…cabin," she muttered, squinting down hard at it. The watermark under the writing shimmered in the uncertain light—*Exelon Nuclear: Clean Energy is the Key to a Brighter Future!* "It's really hard to see in here. I wish we could turn on the lights. I wish we *had* lights." She freed up her other hand and ran a finger along the note's meandering top and bottom edges. "Why did they use a torn-up piece of paper? I bet they could have written us more if they'd used a bigger one."

"They were probably in a hurry." Mia gently pried it from Sherry's grasp and carefully refolded it. As she tucked it back into her pocket, her fingers brushed the two other torn, sharp-edged pieces of paper shoved further down inside it. If she closed her eyes, she could see their kitchen now on the darkness behind her eyelids, just as clearly as if she was sitting there instead on here. Just as it had been four—five—six days ago? She had lost track of exactly how many days.

Their kitchen…and Sherry, sitting at the breakfast table with a Pop-Tart clutched in one hand, staring up at the TV: "Mommy forgot to leave it on YouTube. This is the *Weather Channel*," grumpily. "What's a 'solar flare?' And she said that's for you, it has your name on it." A big yellow envelope sprinkled with Pop-Tart crumbs, resting beside Sherry's elbow. The note inside had been whole then, not yet torn into three separate pieces, two of which must be hidden from Sherry at all costs.

The note—

Mia.

We love you very, very much. As soon as you finish reading this, start packing. The envelope has a list of everything you should try to take with you, along with some maps and the keys to the Jeep. After you get the Jeep loaded—

"Remember?" Sherry asked suddenly, twisting around so she could look up at Mia's face, startling her back into the present. "Remember, when I was five and we came up here with Rose and Bradley?" She frowned. "Or maybe I was six. But we brought our iPads and then we couldn't get a signal so we just played hide and seek instead—so I guess it's okay that you wouldn't let me bring my iPad." She sighed. "Did Uncle William take Rose and Bradley somewhere else?"

"I hope so," Mia meant to say, but her throat closed and nothing came out.

Don't go looking for anyone. Don't stop for anyone. However far you've got by noon tomorrow, just park the Jeep there, get out and start walking, as fast as you can. Don't bring anything electronic with you. Search your and your sister's pockets and packs and make sure you have nothing electronic in them, this is VERY VERY IMPORTANT, MIA.

"Mia? What's wrong?"

"Nothing. Just a cramp."

If your dad and I aren't at the cabin waiting for you, I'm so sorry and so is your dad, he can't even look at what I'm writing now. Please don't come anywhere near the city looking for us, please. We're going to try to come to you, I swear. I love you and Sherry so so much, please give your sister our love every day and never forget how much we love you.

Scratching sounds came from the still-ajar cabin door, followed by the pup squeezing back in through the gap. Sherry jumped up and ran to him, scooping up his now-soaked little body in her arms and kissing him while he frantically licked her chin. Mia's eyes prickled and her breath hitched in her chest—but Sherry might glance back at her at any minute. She scrubbed her forearm viciously hard across her face instead and shoved herself to her feet, crossing the cabin to the door.

The breeze from outside was damp and cool. Mia inhaled deeply, then stopped in mid-breath, fingers clenching hard around the doorframe. There was a faint, acrid tang to the air; she pressed her forehead hard against the edge of the door and peered out past the impenetrable tangle of treetops stretching down the mountainside.

Your dad and I have to go back to the plant and make sure that everything is shut down and the control room circuitry disassembled, as much as we can. Even if the electrical fires after the corona hits blaze out of control, if we can isolate the reactor core, it might not be affected.

The huge, arching bowl of the sky above was bright, pearlescent gray; the remnants of the auroras that had writhed across it in an eerily silent, ceaseless riot of color for the past three nights still flickered on the skyline. Like a reversal of the dawn, a thick black haze was creeping sullenly upward from the distant horizon to mingle with the retreating storm clouds.

Take the very best care you can of yourself and your sister.

Use the guns if you have to.

Please.

I love you.

Mom

Behind her, Sherry laughed delightedly and the coydog pup barked, a sweet high yipping cry—Mia stepped back and pushed the cabin door shut on the world outside.

⸻ ⬦ ⸻

Lisa Short is a Texas-born, Kansas-bred writer of fantasy, science fiction and horror. She has an honorable discharge from the United States Army, a degree in chemical engineering, and twenty years' experience as a professional engineer. Lisa currently lives in Maryland with her husband, youngest child, father-in-law and cat.

In the Wake of the Storm

Alex Shvartsman

I watch fragments of someone else's life float in several feet of cold water.

The sun shines through the basement window, illuminating the water. Much of it has receded on its own, leaving a high-water line at nearly six feet. What remains is a muddy, wet mess with debris floating on the surface.

There's a black and white photo within arm's reach. I set the hose down on the staircase steps, reach down, and scoop it up from the bottom. The paper is too soggy after spending nearly two days in the water. Smiling strangers stare at me for the last time and the photograph comes apart in my hand.

If I could access my magic, I'd drain the water with a wave of my hand, dry out the walls and floors, and kill the mold spores with a mere thought. Instead, I'm forced to do things the hard way.

I lower the hose into the water until it reaches the carpet, and begin to pump. The Shop-Vac is hooked to a portable generator outside, and it sure beats filling a bucket by hand, but this is a home model capable of holding only a few gallons at a time. I empty the container onto the sodden grass in the backyard over and over again.

An old man sits on the plastic chair outside, wrapped in several layers of sweaters and a long coat with a mud-soaked hem. He watches the volunteers scramble to save the lower level of his home. Someone asks him if he has a place to stay. It'll get very cold tonight and most of Far Rockaway, Queens is still without heat and power. The old man doesn't respond at first. He stares past us, lost in his thoughts. When the question is repeated, he says he'll be fine, that he'd been through worse when he was deployed in Korea.

I return downstairs and continue to work. I plow through exhaustion and back pain. Each bucket of water emptied onto the lawn is an offering, a penance, a punishment. Locked away somewhere deep within me there is power enough to avert a hurricane. I should have found a way to reach it, to tame it. But I failed to summon my magic and could do nothing more than watch as the water surge battered the city. Everything that happened, the devastation around me, the old man haunted by a lifetime of memories he lost in the storm, and thousands more like him--all of that is my fault.

I see her for the first time when the new volunteers arrive. I'm dragging garbage bags to the curb when a group of them walks down the beach block, their clothes still clean. I catch a glimpse of her blond curly hair and slight build and, for a brief moment, I think she's Anne. I am jolted with the shock of it and look closer, study her face, and realize my mistake. She doesn't even look all that much like Anne , but I can't stop stealing glances at her.

Information is easy to come by among the volunteers. We talk during smoke breaks and other brief moments of rest, eager for human contact, anxious to push the tragedy around us from the forefront of our minds. Although her group is working further down the block, within a few hours I learn that her name is Tara and she isn't local. She's with some nonprofit out of Florida and they travel around the country to assist people after natural disasters. Hurricane Sandy is the first event her group has been dispatched to in the North East.

We call it a day around four in the afternoon. The sun is already setting and it'll be dark within the hour. Our group is packing up for the day when I hear a commotion down the block.

Two men, one a resident, the other a volunteer from the looks of it, are in each other's faces. I can't hear the words, but their anger and frustration are clear enough. I don't know what caused their argument. Tensions are running high and everyone is on edge. From the body language and facial expressions, it's likely that things are about to come to blows.

For what must be the hundredth time today, I concentrate as hard as I can and try to summon my spark. Even the tiniest bit of power would be enough to calm their minds, to prevent this small ugliness from piling on to the misery caused by the storm. I search for the spark, but there's nothing. I walk toward them, hoping to get there quickly enough, hoping that I can figure out some way to diffuse the situation without magic.

Tara gets there first.

She inserts her five-foot frame between the two much larger men without hesitation. She speaks to them, too softly for me to hear, with a half-smile on her face. Her words must be even better than my magic. In the time it takes me to get near, the two men are visibly calmer, almost subdued. I stop a few steps away and watch, fearful of breaking whatever truce Tara had managed to conjure up.

The one I took for a resident looks almost embarrassed. He offers his hand to the other man and they shake. Then he nods to Tara and walks off to his house. The other man heads toward his group of friends. Then there's just Tara, standing in the middle of the street. She winces and massages her left temple, and just as I'm about to turn back, I feel the tiniest shift in my mind. For the first time in weeks, I feel the spark.

The spark flickers within me like an electrical short, barely there. Not enough to do major magic. Not enough to help with the devastation that surrounds me. But maybe, just maybe, it's enough to alleviate this one woman's headache. I exhale, a small puff of breath visible in the rapidly cooling air, concentrate, and reach into her head.

Her mind is closed off, hidden behind mental barriers I've never encountered before. She looks up sharply and stares at me. *This isn't supposed to happen.* Magic is subtle, unnoticeable to regular people. All they can ever experience directly is the outcome. And yet she notices. Her eyes widen with recognition as she stares into mine. As I come to a realization, I'm certain she does as well.

She and I are the same.

We sit in my car, the engine idling to keep the heat on, and we talk.

Neither of us has ever met another practitioner before. I've always known that others were out there. I felt traces of their magic, outcomes of spells good and bad, immense tragedies and uplifting miracles. But never a direct encounter. Never like this.

She tells me about her life in Orlando. An ordinary life, devoid of magic and strangeness. Twenty-two years of normalcy, until the brain tumor.

She tells me about the time spent in hospitals, the difficult and ultimately successful surgery to remove the tumor, and the slow, painful recovery through a haze of sterile rooms and white lab coats. It was then that she first discovered her abilities, her power to do wondrous things, likely gained through some improbable side effect of the surgery. Plentiful magic, always at her command, letting her work all kinds of miracles, do almost anything, except make her headaches go away.

She tells me about long hours spent in hospital beds, reevaluating her life. How she wanted to use her newfound gift to give something back, to help reduce the suffering of others. About her last visit to New York, after 9/11, her time in New Orleans post-Katrina, her stint abroad in Yuriage, Japan after the 2008 tsunami.

My life isn't nearly as interesting, but I tell her about it anyway. I tell her about growing up with this power, confused and frightened by it, and never quite in control. One moment I feel like a demigod, strong enough to move mountains, to topple governments, to do almost anything at all, but the next minute it's gone. My magic is absent when a hurricane bears down on the city that has become my home, on my friends and neighbors. What good is power if it isn't there when you really need it?

I tell her about Anne. The only person to whom I've ever been close enough, trusted enough, to tell about my power. Anne understood. She never asked me to use magic on her behalf, never blamed me when I couldn't find the spark. We were happy together. And then her mother grew ill. We watched helplessly as cancer ate at her mother's body, as she wasted away in a matter of months.

I wanted desperately to help her, to save her, to take away even a little of her pain. But the spark had abandoned me. I hadn't felt its presence in months, and no amount of wishing would bring it back.

Anne was strong. She knew I was trying. She knew I wanted to help. But everyone has their limit, and Anne reached hers in her mother's final days. She lashed out at me, screaming, accusing me of murder by inaction, demanding that I find a way to summon my power and purge the metastasized cancer cells from her mother's body.

Then I tell Tara the difficult part. I want to keep it hidden, but I find myself unable to lie to her, even by omission. So I allow her to see me for the coward I really am. I confess to running away. To leaving Anne behind, because I couldn't help her mother, and because I couldn't stand to see her in pain. She might have forgiven me, in time, but I'd always imagine the accusation, even when it was no longer there.

So I ran. I left Anne, and I left San Antonio. I moved to New York City and lived an unglamorous life of waiting for those brief moments when the spark would flare up within me, and I would become more than a fraction of myself.

We talk for hours, and it feels like catching up with an old, dear friend rather than a stranger I met this afternoon. Neither of us wants to stop, but a day of physical labor has taken its toll. We're exhausted and hungry.

I drive across the bridge and take Belt Parkway into Brooklyn. Less than twenty minutes later we're in Bay Ridge, a neighborhood that was largely unaffected by the storm. It feels like another world. There are lights, bars and restaurants are open, and groups of young people laugh as they stroll down the sidewalks not covered in mud and sand.

We wolf down some sandwiches and then drive to my studio apartment in Bensonhurst. There, we undress each other and allow our bodies and our minds to intertwine. Our lovemaking feels like the most natural thing in the world--there is none of the pressure, none of the urgency of a typical first encounter. In this, too, we feel like long-lost soul mates, reconnected at last.

We don't bother showing up on our designated block the following morning. Not because we shirk from helping people--far from it. We discover that, together, we can do so much more. Tara's presence acts as some sort of amplifier, fanning the flames of my magic beyond anything I've been capable of before.

The next few days are a blur. We walk the streets of Far Rockaway and Breezy Point, Canarsie and Seagate, and we bestow anonymous blessings like a pair of traveling angels.

We lift spirits and cool tempers. We mend foundations of homes that would be condemned otherwise, and prevent sinkholes from forming under the streets. And we cure people, purging ailments they don't even know they have, shrinking cancers and clearing arteries, lifting depressions. We can't be everywhere at once, aren't powerful enough to help everyone-- but we make things incrementally better wherever we go, and that's enough.

Tara's headaches are epic and my magic is there to help soothe them, a mending she couldn't work on herself. When I'm with her, my power is reliably there, and while I can't shake the fear of losing it at a crucial moment after so many years of uncertainty, I'm finding it very easy to get used to its constant presence.

Together, we're happy.

Even with the two of us enhancing each other's powers, there are limits to what we can accomplish. By the end of the day we're exhausted, wrung out like a wet towel. We share a comfortable silence as we wait in a protracted gas line. It stretches on for several blocks, and it takes my car over two hours to inch up to within sight of the station.

Outside, there is a somewhat shorter line for people with gas cans. Forty minutes of freezing outdoors gets you up to five gallons of gasoline. We watch a woman carry a full red canister away from the station like some prized possession, when a man jumps out from the shadows, snatches her canister, and runs.

I search for the spark, trying to summon my magic in time to help. The spark is there but almost dormant, my power spent throughout the day. Then I feel Tara's anger. It feeds my spark in a wholly different way and fans it into a brilliant burning flame. Her rage is like lighter fluid poured generously onto the fire of my ability. Despite the urgency, I take a moment to revel in so much power, and then I act.

The thief stumbles and goes down, rough concrete scraping his hands and face. He recoils from the horrors I inserted into his mind's eye. I conjure fears from the deepest corners of his self, his worst nightmares given shape. Then he howls and runs, pursued by phantoms.

I struggle not to do a lot worse. But using magic to cause fear and pain isn't the path I want to travel. Instead, I enjoy the euphoria of extra power even as it drains away from me. There's just enough left to assuage Tara's headache.

We don't pay attention to the news, since we're busy helping people, doing stuff that's actually important. Because of this, I don't learn about the next storm until it's almost upon us.

This one is called a nor'easter instead of a hurricane, but it's malevolent and powerful, and I can feel traces of dark magic in every gust of its icy wind.

I let Tara know that something bad is coming on the heels of the previous storm. Something that's potentially as bad as Sandy. And then I tell her that she and I should stop it. She balks at the challenge. She believes that, even together, our powers aren't enough to tackle something on this scale. But I won't be dissuaded. I won't hold back, not this time, not when I'm able to access my power.

I believe that storms like this are no accident of nature. There must be evil men out there using their power to strengthen the storms. To aim them at major cities, to hurl them at where they can do the most damage, to cause misery, and pain, and death. I can sense their subtle machinations whenever my own spark cooperates.

If there are people out there evil and powerful enough to control the storms, then such magic can be undone by humans as well. We may or may not be powerful enough to do it, but I argue that we owe it to the millions of people in our city to try.

Reluctantly, she agrees to help me.

We make several attempts, none successful.

With Tara's help I can reach into the heart of the storm. I can see its inner workings and feel the medley of raw energy and dark magics that power it. But I'm not strong enough to alter its path, to dampen its fury. It feels like trying to move a very large piece of furniture on my own. I might be able to handle the weight if only there was a good way to grab proper hold of it.

Tara wants to give up. Her headache flares up, so much so that I can't soothe it with my magic. My heart breaks at her suffering, but I know that the two of us must work through it, pay any price, in order to succeed. I know what I have to do.

I say unkind, hurtful things in order to urge her on. I hate myself and vow to apologize later, to make amends. But Tara's anger is the key; it is the only way to achieve the extra power boost I need. So I force myself to remember the things Anne threw in my face as her mother lay dying in the cancer ward, and I repeat them to Tara. I accuse her of not wanting to help, or being selfish and cruel, of not loving me enough to give it her all.

Her hurt and anger feed my spark until there is an inferno raging within me. I have more power than I've ever imagined myself wielding. So much power that, for a moment, I fear it will incinerate me from the inside if I don't find an outlet for it soon.

I unleash my power on the heart of the storm. My mind untangles the Gordian knot of dark magics, brushes aside the web of incantations binding and directing the storm, and soothes the worst of the natural patterns that drive it. I am like some ancient weather god, laughing as I ride the wind.

It is only as the power begins to drain from me that I turn my attention to Tara. She lies on the floor, unconscious, blood trickling from a nostril. The sight of her suffering jolts me back to reality, brings me crashing down from the supernatural high. I want so badly to make her better. Perhaps I can use what's left of the power boost to cure her of her migraines, once and for all.

I look inside of her mind and withdraw in shock and shame. Tara's headaches are not the side effect of the brain surgery. They're the price she pays for her magic.

Unlike Tara, I grew up with my power. It has been unreliable and frustrating, not always there when I wanted it, but it has never exacted a physical cost. In my incredible arrogance, I assumed that's how it worked for everyone.

Tara has much greater control over her spark, but she pays a price. The more magic she uses, the worse her headaches become. My desire to be a hero didn't merely drain her. It almost killed her.

I tend to Tara, check her vital signs, clean up the blood and drag her over to the bed. I do what I can to heal her, to make her comfortable, until the last shreds of magic drain away. I feel small, insignificant. Human. I plow through the nausea and fight the urge to black out.

Tara's breathing is a little labored, but steady. Careful not to wake her, I grab my jacket and go outside.

Gentle snow is falling on New York City. The nor'easter, robbed of its supernatural boost, has become just another day of bad weather, a calamity no one will recall. Tara and I have succeeded.

I walk the streets, ignoring the cold and the snow. My thoughts keep racing back to the moment I looked inside of Tara's mind. I didn't just mimic Anne when I lashed out at Tara with hurtful words. I became Anne. I demanded more magic of Tara than she could stand to conjure but, unlike me, Tara was strong enough to make the sacrifice. To give more of herself than I had any right to ask.

I never quite forgave Anne for her outburst. How could I hope that Tara would forgive me? I left Anne. Surely, Tara will leave me too, once she recovered and had

time to reflect. Surely, she will not be able to look at me the same way, ever again.

Last time, I ran because Anne's words hurt me almost as much as my inability to act hurt her. This time, running would be a kindness. I can spare Tara any guilt of leaving me, if I leave her first.

I wander the snow-covered sidewalks without a purpose. Tears mix with melted snowflakes on my cheeks.

My entire life, magic has been my gift and my curse. I've been careful to use it only to do good, tried to make the world around me a better place. But I've also been a coward. I've allowed my power to keep me from trusting people. Used it as an excuse to erect barriers and to end relationships. I told myself that it was a part of me no one could understand. Until I met Tara and she changed everything.

This time, I dare not run away. I don't want to hurt Tara. I would rather cut off my arm; I'd rather never use magic again, then to cause her any more pain. I cling to the hope that she might be able to forgive me, because she is a better person than I.

Tara might leave me anyway. She might walk out cursing my name, and I'll understand. But I must let the choice be hers. I will be there for her, if she'll have me. I come up the stairs to my apartment, my body shivering from cold and anticipation, and I open the door.

Alex Shvartsman is a writer, translator, and anthologist from Brooklyn, NY. He's the author of The Middling Affliction (2022) and Eridani's Crown (2019) fantasy novels. Over 120 of his short stories have appeared in Analog, Nature, Strange Horizons, and many other venues. His website is www.alexshvartsman.com.

You Blossoms of Their Seeds

Renan Bernardo

You never fucked a man in your life. Yet, you're pregnant.

The gynecologist's office crimps around you, lustrous white walls pulsing with ovaries, wombs, and tiny, uncomfortable numbers that tell you nothing about your condition. The doctor herself is as slim as you, fragrant with grapes and traces of disbelief, glasses hanging on the tip of her nose.

Your fingers hover above your watch's pre-defined messages for Julia. Kisses. I love you. I'll be right there. Not one of them condenses what you feel within, that feeling of how the hell you're pregnant if you never stuck a dick inside you or performed artificial insemination. You're not even religious to be Mary's second coming.

The answer comes two days later, wearing austere suits and medical coats. You're home with Julia, a seat between you on the three-place sofa, dust filtering through the curtains, picking out the sunlight and the tears you've been sucking in.

Women are conceiving without sexual intercourse.

The initial shock is washed in bland suppositions. A virus, God's miracle and revenge, mutation, alien schemes, apocalypse. Only twelve days later there's something you can grasp: spores now pervade the world, inadvertently discharged by men's bodies.

You stand and hug Julia, her neck bristling with the sweet watermelon shampoo of her shower, your bellies tight against each other. You caress, rub, press your lover's back so she knows you're going through this unplanned madness together. You share the sofa's middle seat and discuss abortion, hands crisscrossed upon each other, yours warm and quivery, hers as cold and static as her gaze on you. *You decide,* Julia says. It's your body and your body only, no matter how much of it you share every night.

And you want the child. You know you do. You always did, just not under the world's unwitting terms.

When darkness lurks through the flat, as it inevitably does, you think, whisper, speak with a loud, shaken voice scarring night and sleep, *You can get it too, but you shouldn't.* Julia's mitral valve is narrow. If she gets pregnant, it might lead to her heart's failure. With her voice cracked in between insomniac tears, she tells you to rest assured, the treatment will come as fast as anything when men are also affected. But when lightness drips through the curtains, you're sitting against the headboard, a hand folded around Julia's wrist, feeling her pulsing on your fingers.

At noon, over coffee, toast, and the indistinct hum of a new world outside, you bring hysterectomy and open-heart surgery to the table. Either way, Julia has to gouge out part of herself, to deliver part of her as a tithe. Otherwise, she might not survive when the tiny speckles aim to seed her.

But when the first month passes, you find out you're all out of options. Nothing would keep her safe. The spores bring all sorts of adverse symptoms to most women who can't be inseminated. Hypotension, strokes, blood clots, thrombosis... Heart failure. It's the spores' contraceptive vengeance, as if they need to chastise you if they can't bloat you with their seeds. In due time, all women in childbearing age will either be impregnated or will have to face the consequences.

As the boy swells in you, your back bows to it in crushing, captive pain. All around, many things swarm fast into reality. Pregnancy test apps, spore detectors, filters, spore-killing sprays, doubtful protection amulets. Two words clog the news. Mother, woman, mother, woman, mother. Scientific articles abound. *An analysis of fertility and the risks of becoming spored. Methods to detect DNA changes in spore children. The rise of women cooperatives in pursuit of a healthy work environment.*

Some numbers soar. Religious cults. Single mothers. Child abandonment. But no treatment comes.

You and Julia are working double shift when men-women voluntary apartheid is announced. Filter cities emerge almost overnight to accommodate women who opt to stay away from men's invisible, invasive touch.

And you meet Julia for lunch when the first city is inaugurated. The tepid wind blows through the park and plucks at your dress, roily life prickling underneath it. You see Julia from a distance, mind whirling with how many spores might be invisibly pimpling the air around her, wafting to reach her and wring her heart from you. The first thing you notice when you clasp her hands is she doesn't clasp yours back. Instead, she glares at you, dark blue lipstick fluttering. Because she knows what you'll say. With Julia, your words travel ahead of you, every letter a microscopic, verbal particle yet unsaid. *You want me to go,* she stutters.

It's the only way to keep her protected, and it's only until you can sort things out, until the world finds a solution. You clamp your hands together, praying for her comprehension. She tells you she wants to see the birth. She wants to bundle the boy in her arms. It's her right. He's as much hers as he's yours. She asks, cries, begs for you to come with her at least, but you can't. As soon as the child is born, he'll strew both of you with spores, and even if they're not mature to inseminate a woman, they're ripe to exact their revenge. With gritty teeth, tears beading on dark blue, she accuses you of ripping off her motherhood. You're steadfast, though. You play on her feelings, poking them despite the remorse, like a torturer forced to do their grisly job. You tear yourself from the inside out when you tell her you won't deprive her of visiting the boy, it's temporary. You just want to reduce the probability. You'll never want the boy to grow up without one of his mothers, but you can't let her die. This isn't supposed to be sacrifice.

When you arrive from work that night, you arrive to her clove and musk, the perfume you gave her on your fifth anniversary. The bed's barren and tidy, the left-side dresser empty but for a matte, scratched mirror that barely reflects your messy face. You strip off your dress and shrink on the bed, breathing, suffocating, drowning in Julia's scent.

You lose your job a few days before Dan is born. They can't keep you now that you'll have a child to take care of and the possibility of being impregnated again. They politely and sympathetically recommend you to search for one of the women cooperatives. You've grown too large, excessively risky, your belly bearing down their stocks. You affectionately open your best grin and tell them to fuck off.

The next morning, as you roll down through job listings, your watch vibrates. Julia's face floats there, tiny, unreachable. Call Julia, Text Julia, Locate Julia, it suggests, unaware you don't talk since your meeting at the park. You sniff, inhale, savor the air, longing for her clove, her musk, the aftertaste of her dark blue lips. But you get nothing except exhaustion.

In the feeble light of your flat, dimmed by the building in front of it, it all crashes on you. Your harshness, your evil, your grit to rip away a mother from her child. And you realize you're but a purposeless single mother wading through life. And amidst the dust and staleness of the flat, and the sickening light of your laptop's screen, you'd give anything to pull Julia back at your side, to share the same seat with her and have her hands over your belly, delicately tracing the line from your chest to your navel. Thoughts crunch you as you think on how you could've done differently, how you sacrificed the only person who ever murmured words of affection to you for an infinitesimal mite of life that violated your body.

You tap your watch and call her, eyes blurry, the flat distorted. But she doesn't answer. The only thing you know about her is she really went to live in one of the spore-free women complexes, in a secluded, filtered area, out of reach from the walking flowers that were men, far from their forest of impregnation and unsuspecting pain.

You're so muddled and anesthetized by your thoughts that it's your watch that tells you when your water breaks that night.

Dan is born surrounded by hazmat-protected doctors. He has your lips and your plump, speckled nose. His eyes gleam in foreign apricot. As you snuggle with him, his minute fingers tickling the skin of your neck, you realize the two of you are incomplete, and a cord still extends far from there, uncut, leading to the whole of you.

You decide to follow that cord.

You find out in the filter city's gate that Julia doesn't live there anymore. Many women left. The city doesn't work as expected. The spores travel far and wide, like sand from the Sahara, but with spermatozoic insistence in thriving.

An old woman comes from the gate, smelling of sylvan gardens, and gently pulls your elbow. *Is it Julia Ribeiro you're searching for?* Ribeiro. Your name. She still uses it even after you banned her. The woman smiles when she sees Dan on your arms, but grimaces when she tells you what you don't want to hear. Julia's been admitted to a hospital a few days ago. And you don't want to know why yet. You just want to know where. You just need to be with her, to kneel beside her and ask, cry, beg for her pardon. But the old woman speaks.

It's something to do with her baby.

You can't remember, and never will, how you got to the hospital. From the moment you arrived in the waiting room for the rest of your life, you'll just believe you evanesced from the filter city's entrance with Dan cuddled in your arms, both of you turning into wispy smoke and materializing in the hospital.

They're going to open Julia's heart and try to save her and the baby. Odds are not good. The doctor spills out uncomfortable numbers that tell you nothing about her condition. Before your thoughts can resettle, you're alone. Again. A women-child bubble in an empty waiting room smelling of antiseptic despair. You pat Dan's forehead, numb to his eager sucking on your breast. He giggles and stretches his tiny fingers, unaware one of his mothers is alone—*abandoned*—at the other side of a thick wall. Somewhere, in a faraway reality, a TV speaks words of universal basic income, shared paternity, mandatory nurseries, taxes for men.

You also won't remember when you go home and come back, one day later, after the doctor told you Julia wouldn't discharge from the hospital yet. In your mind, you've remained in the waiting room, you and Dan, one enveloping the other in amniotic hope. He, staring at you. You, staring at the double door that leads to the surgery room, the cord linking the … three of you.

Julia leaves accompanied by a doctor, pacing slowly in a fading beige hospital gown. She's slim, pale, lips slightly blue but not of lipstick. You picture yourself cupping her chin and gently kissing her, but you don't move. After all you've done, you can't. She eyes Dan, teary-eyed, and plucks him out of your arms. The doctor wants to say something, to give any news she has to give. Instead, she nods at you and leaves.

When Julia's eyes pan from Dan to you, your lips quiver with dryness. Her cheeks dimple in the stern lines you deserve. She knows what you're unable to turn into words. *Yes, I forgive you,* she says.

It takes a year for Julia's heart to fully recover. A year for you to deserve her smile again. A year for the spore treatment.

You and Julia are sitting on opposite sides of the sofa. Dan crawls on the floor, giggling toothlessly at you. He grapples with the sofa's edge and tries to pull himself up. Yes, he's not all you, not all yours. He has her resilience…

You grab him and pull him up, snuggling him on the middle seat. A three-knotted cord. You kiss his head and sniff his pudgy neck. He also has her clove and musk.

Renan Bernardo is a science fiction and fantasy writer from Rio de Janeiro, Brazil. His fiction appeared or is forthcoming in Apex Magazine, Podcastle, Dark Matter Magazine, Daily Science Fiction, Translunar Travelers Lounge, Solarpunk Magazine, The Dread Machine, and others. He was one of the selected for the 2021 Imagine 2200 climate fiction contest with his story When It's Time to Harvest. In Brazil, he was a finalist for two important SFF awards and published multiple stories. His fiction has also appeared in other languages.

The Wyldblood 10ᵗʰ issue 10 Best lists

10 best science fiction TV

Battlestar Galactica (remake)
Stranger Things
Fringe
Snowpiercer
The Expanse
Star Trek: Strange New Worlds
The 100
Orphan Black
Stargate Universe
The OA

10 Best Fantasy Films

The Lord of the Rings: The Fellowship
of the Ring
Stardust
Pan's Labyrinth
The Wizard of Oz
Crouching Tiger, Hidden Dragon
The Chronicles of Narnia: The Lion,
the Witch and the Wardrobe
Jumanji: Welcome to the Jungle
The Princess Bride
Coraline
The Weight of Water

10 best fantasy novels

The lord of the Rings – J.R.R Tolkein
A Game of Thrones – George R.R. Martin
Good Omens – Neil Gaiman and Terry Pratchett
The colour of magic – Terry Pratchett
Cloud Atlas – David Mitchell
The Fifth Season – N.K. Jemsin
Under the Pendulum Sun – Jeanette Ng
Northern lights - Phillip Pullman
The Earthsea Trilogy – Ursula LeGuin
Perdido Street Station – China Miéville

A Plea, Eleven Minutes Before the Final Divine Act of the Century

Brandon R Chinn

Valverde turns her communications channel on eleven minutes before she's going to die. It's a miracle that it works, that the transmission goes through—nearly everything in her cockpit is worthless and fried, gone.

She's one big bruise, a blotchy painting in browns and blues, and the mechanical action of flicking the channel sends ripples of pain through her arm. The transmission gutters, crackles, and she's convinced the electronics are obliterated, just as she should be. There is nothing at first—silence plays out in undulating strands, a false ocean that lives in the empty shells down by the beach.

Silence, and then—

"Valverde! Oh my god, oh my god honey you're alive!"

His voice—shot from yelling commands through the bloodbath—is so sweet it dances across her skin. It's the voice that's calmed her anger countless times as she lay on their veranda with a glass of blackberry moonshine, so fresh that it strips her insides. The voice that convinced her there was a livelihood in the service. The last thing she hears before she falls asleep every night.

"It's me, darling. It's me."

Mercifully the software is still working, and the automated cough button interjects as she spits blood and hacks up pieces of dislodged gut. Valverde doesn't even bother to wipe it away, and thinks about cracking a joke about last night's dinner—her husband has never really been inoculated to her bad sense of humor, and wouldn't take kindly to the knowledge that he burned her last meal.

23

Ten minutes remain until Valverde's death, and her sweet Nehan doesn't know it.

"I'm so happy to hear your voice. They've confirmed the kill—the last leviathan is dead. You can turn around. You can come home!"

She blinks at that news. Blood and sweat sting her eyes.

Valverde is trying not to look at her other hand, the one mangled in its metal sleeve, the one that guided her machine's spear into the heart of the monstrous whale. It was perfect and now it's abstract, never to be a hand again.

"It was a hell of a fight," she says, and smiles through the pain. "I used grandpa's manoeuvre. I almost didn't want to tell you that. Only something that crazy could have kept me alive."

The line is quiet for too long. She blinks tiredly at the black screen, its face striated with cracks. Barely an hour ago that screen was filled with the faces of her dear comrades, their victory a certainty. It never works out that way, and she should know that by now.

"I'll go down to his plot and kiss the fucking headstone."

His tone is guarded. It's cute, knowing that a dozen other people are listening on the line. Still, it feels like they are the last ones in the universe drifting on a vast and endless ocean, each without a body.

Valverde hesitates. There are nine minutes left and she doesn't know how she's going to tell him.

In another life—both years ago and yesterday—they fell in love between rows of wheat on a strip of land that had been barren only one hundred years before. Their families weren't military—that generation was long gone, replaced by a newly sparked network of agricultural motivations. They lived in elysian fields and dreamed their dreams with calloused palms and green thumbs.

Valverde grew up with her grandfather's history, passed down by father and father and father, of their emancipation from commercial misery. She sat on the ruins of ancient cities and climbed in the cold buckets of old war machines. A young Valverde long dreamed of touching the clouds, her hands on the reconstructed pommels of technology lost to time.

She had done it, and now eight minutes remained.

"Nehan, my love, listen to me. My systems don't have much longer."

"You're right. We'll talk more when you return home. I bet your machine looks like shit. We'll get the old girl fixed up."

It's a broken nest of glass and steel and wires, the cockpit miraculously staying closed but chattering like teeth in winter. Hell is the place where you lose your arm and both your legs beneath two tons of living armor, where your final moments are pressed into a steel cocoon that's flying through a pink sky at a thousand miles an hour.

Hell is having only a few minutes left to tell your husband goodbye and stalling, because you can't bear for him to walk through this world alone.

Valverde reaches for the first aid bag, comically undamaged. The machine is on autopilot now; there is only one way for it to go. In seven minutes, she will arrive at the nest, to finish this once and for all.

She reaches into the bag, shakes the contents across her lap, and finds a painkiller. Her undamaged hand swaying like a tender tomato plant against the first chill winds of autumn, she grasps the morphine and downs the bottle. It's all she has, and it will get her through the next few minutes.

A blanket mixture of sweat and blood clouds her vision while Nehan is peppering questions through the comm.

"Honey? Why haven't you turned back? Is something wrong with your navigation? Touch down and we'll send the rescue crew."

They went on their first date three years ago. Her grandfather sat on the porch all night. When they walked up together in the morning's waning hours hand in hand, the old man was slumped over, snoring so loud that it frightened the hounds. Valverde tucked a quilt over the rough soldier and pecked Nehan on the cheek and sent him off through the fields.

Valverde and Nehan shared their first kiss mere feet from her childhood home, framed by wheat and corn and barley, the breeze scented with the earthen freshness of tomato plants and squash blossoms. As they retreated from the kiss, Valverde grinned to see the depth of his timorous personality. He would always be that way, blushing over a squeeze or bashfully recoiling from a sudden kiss on the cheek.

It was only one year later when they walked off her grandfather's porch arm in arm, surrounded by cheering and crying family that tossed petals in the air. It became their home after the old man's death, a place enshrined in family memories and generational baubles. Their home smelled like dogs and soil—it smelled like a life well lived.

"Nehan. I'm not coming back."

She gives him time to grieve. The silence is broken; it doesn't take long. The sun is setting, the gloaming is at the peak of its colors where emerald is washed through the gold and salmon—if she could see her machine streaking across the sky as she is, Valverde would be surprised by the untouched wings, miraculously undamaged. She's all folded up now, a paper plane, an arrow launching through time and space to strike one final target.

Her husband speaks, says: "Why does it have to be you?"

Valverde doesn't know how to answer that. What is there to say that isn't pained, that isn't obvious against their circumstances? Nehan already knows. The last few miles were littered with the pieces of people she loved. Why does she have to say it aloud?

The ruined remains of their squadron will be collected in the morning. Crews will walk and drive all one hundred-fifty-three miles of the battlefield and scour the ruin for what can be re-purposed. Children as young as nine will pick at the metal corpses with gloved hands, their collective breath like dragon's smoke, the ground hard with frost. New machines will be built, their insignias saved, and dead names will be carved inside of metal plates and beneath wings and on dashboards. Amalgamations will streak the sky, artifacts that were pieces of your neighbor and your uncle and your grandmother, bolted together.

"It should be me," says the intercom, her husband's voice. Nehan's trying not to shake, his words thick with unshed tears. He cried on their wedding night. He cried when they planted their first garden together.

"You're a shit pilot, hon."

A break in the line. Static. The connection comes back in, but the nearer she gets to the nest, the worse the fuzz will be. Soon she will be divorced from the world.

"Tomorrow—"

"Fuck tomorrow."

"Tomorrow, you will do your job. The new pilots will need you. You'll tell everyone about me and what I did, because you're a softy, because you love your wife."

She doesn't want to say the rest. Doesn't want to talk about the philosophies of a wife in the void, of being married to someone who doesn't exist anymore. When her machine reaches the exterior membrane of the nest's armor, when her damaged machine of the union militia transitions from vehicle to bomb, there will no longer be a person known as Lucinda Valverde.

She doesn't know what to do with that, and knows that her husband won't know what to do with it either.

He says: "Turn around, Valverde. Turn the fuck around right now."

They're at six minutes—he hasn't found full panic yet, hasn't thrown up, hasn't screamed. At five minutes, he'll turn into that authority. He'll threaten her. He'll roar. She'll hear the sounds of breaking glass and metal on the other end, of chairs launched across the room.

At four minutes, he'll beg and plead and cry.

Nehan will tell Valverde that he'd rather live in a world plagued by war and suffering with her than live in peace without.

A crack has been growing in the protective forward glass of the machine. Valverde has been watching it carefully over the last few minutes, knowing there's a gambler's chance the crack splinters the windshield before she even reaches the nest. In this scenario she is thrown out of the machine at maximum velocity and spends the last few seconds of her life flying through the air, unbound. Before her machine can spin out of control and collide with the nearby cliffs, Valverde will be a bird, a rain drop, a woman about to die.

The line in the glass splits her world, the halves are opposing dimensions of possibility, reflections of the past and future. On one side she sees only splendor: endless farming fields, houses built from wood and stone, forests sickly from the years but budding green. Beyond this living panorama Valverde sees her grandfather's father's father's ocean, every day fractionally reclaiming a lighter shade of blue. The other half also belongs to the old men: factories rusting from disuse, lakes black with oil, stretches of concrete buckled and broken.

She closes her eyes to all of it, the middle road dark and lonely.

Valverde's name will be added to a long list of esteemed martyrs. They will write her name in a book and etch it on a machine and the sun will rise tomorrow. Nehan will continue on, even when the pain of her loss feels like working acid sloshed across the skin. Valverde can see him. A year from now her husband will be sitting on their porch, not happy but contented, one hand clutching a mug of warm coffee and the other behind the ears of their old hound.

He will walk the farms alone and remark aloud to himself that the tomatoes have never looked so big.

The radio comes back in. Nehan is frantic. He will never beg for his own life this hard.

"I'm not turning around, my love. I'm not turning back."

"That's a fucking *order!*"

"Oh, my sweet and serious husband, screw your orders."

There are no panels left to show her how fast she's going, but she can gauge it by what the velocity is doing to her cheeks. She's a sonic boom in human form, a clap of thunder thrown across potato fields. In three minutes, Lucinda Valverde will collide with the nest's shielding membrane traveling half the speed of a bullet fired from a gun. At such a speed, her machine will create a forward cone of air that will strike the armored skin before she does. It will punch a tunnel through the outer wall with the force of a hydraulic arm and push her quadrupedal vehicle through the nest's guts. She is a living missile made of love.

The missile Valverde will strike the nest's heart, empty of leviathans. The remaining ammunition stored across her machine will ignite and explode, and she will be an invisible warrior making it across enemy lines in a grand and secret game. In a flash of seconds the impossible heat will blacken her bones, and the nest will burn from the inside out. When the superheated pressure boils the interior gases, it will erupt like a long dormant volcano. Alien guts will be found miles away, hanging from pine trees on the tops of mountain ridges.

She can't feel her good hand anymore.

Valverde is barely conscious enough to keep the throttle straight. She hopes to God that she actually strikes the nest. The half and half windshield is filling with smoke. It's smeared black, and she's afforded the tiniest view of the oncoming world through a piece of glass the size of a picture frame.

"Tell me something sweet."

"Do you remember when I taught you to play chess? It was a week after our first date. We used your grandfather's set, the one he carved by hand. You were enamored with the pieces, how they all looked like little animals."

"Of course I remember. I beat you so bad we never played again."

Nehan's voice cracks, sputters through the dying comm. "I swung that game. I let you win."

Silence on the line. Is this it? Is she already gone? How many more minutes can possibly remain? The painkiller has possessed her. Valverde feels like gelatine, and she's having a hard time seeing anything at all. The whole world has transformed into fog—she's no longer flying in a machine, but floating along an exquisite current of air. She's lighter than anything, and impossibly clear.

"Of course you'd showcase your ruthlessness when I'm on my way out. That's just like you."

"I lived a life of concessions, Lucinda. Sometimes winning matters less than a meaningful time."

She laughs, and coughs up blood. Nothing hurts anymore, but she can feel dislodged pieces grinding in her chest.

The gates of heaven are close. Slicked with blood, sweat and oil, she'll slide right through.

"Everyone's going to know I'm a shit commander," says her husband. "Thirty people dead, and I'm only blubbering over you."

"You've always been a terrible commander," Valverde says, breathing heavy. "That was the trade-off, I think, to be the best fucking husband."

Are there regrets? They never did have the kids, even after choosing names. They never moved out of her grandfather's place,

after talking it to death. Nehan will inherit a smelly old hound dog and acres of farm and a generational home. In twenty years, when he retires from exhaustion and heartbreak, he'll spend his time tinkering with an old truck in the backyard. It will take him six months to fix it up. He'll smile when the engine turns over, and he'll sail down the repaired highway with wind in the hair that's left, the dog hanging out the back and barking at the sunset moon.

Most will never experience the heavy silence that exists between two people in love who know there's only two minutes left on Earth. Neither of them knows what to say, so the years speak for them. They're memorizing one another. They're commanding everything they've ever done to return to the surface. They're willing one heart into the other.

In forty years Nehan will be an old man sitting on the porch of the house he never left, an old man who once had a dog and a wife.

The leviathan nest looms. It's both halves of the split windshield, it's the whole world. Valverde can no longer see the brown smear of farmland or blue smear of sky. There is only this tumorous potato lingering in the flat of space. As she nears it—as the machine rattles around her, jostling a numbed and broken body—Valverde's heart swells with something that briefly pushes away the fear.

With thirty seconds left until impact, Nehan says: "I wouldn't exchange a second of what we had. If in that first evening you had told me how it all ends, I still would have reached for your hand."

In those last thirty seconds Valverde is consumed by the mathematics of chance. Everything they fought for, every frustrating moment, every bad crop, every dull machine core, every nightmare launched them toward this exact moment, a missile out of time.

Playing a game, knowing how it ends before the first move.

There is only one thing to say to him, and she says it.

It is finished, and the days pass.

Out of reverence, the pieces of her machine recovered after the destruction will be left where they fell. The biggest piece—one of the wings, intact—will stick out of the earth at a sharp angle, a monument.

For years, people will gather on the anniversary of her sacrifice to lay flowers and baskets of crop. They will decorate that piece of wing with knits and carved gourds. When the seasons change, and the moss overgrows the metal, and the monument becomes only a thing with a plaque, children will play in its shadow. A hundred years from now when a new city is built over the ruins of the last battle with the leviathans, a property builder will place a glass case over the wing, healthy with green moss, and it will remain there until the end of the next century.

For now—only seconds after impact, when the line is dead and no amount of hysterical repetition can summon an answer—there is a man alone in an empty room weeping over the loss of his wife.

Brandon R. Chinn is the author of the Kognition Cycle. He has pieces featured in Moonchild Magazine, Twist in Time, Selene Quarterly, The Other Stories podcast and the anthology Today, Tomorrow, Always. He writes video games essays at SUPERJUMP. He lives in the Pacific Northwest. You can check out his work at TheKognitionCycle.com and geek out with him @brandonrchinn on Twitter.

Love in the Apocalypse

It was Beautiful

M.A. Dosser

The pneumatic tube arrived with a clunk. Inside was a scrap of crumpled newspaper the length of my thumb. On it, Rufus had scribbled, "Did you see the sunrise?"

My bunker had access cameras, but I hadn't checked them in years. The nuclear winter felt never-ending. Clouds of ash still blanketed the sky. I hadn't seen a sunrise since the attack.

Rufus knew that. That's not why he asked.

There was so much I wanted to say to him, but there was no space. We were almost out of paper. Almost out of time.

"Yes," I wrote, "It was beautiful."

Superstar

Marilee Dahlman

Call me a diva if you want, but nobody understands what really happened that night. The situation arose at dress rehearsal. Nothing at stake except money from all the billionaire donors in the moon-base audience. The big event, the one that all life on Earth depended on, was scheduled for the next evening. We needed to impress those newly-arrived creatures. Convince them we were sufficiently exceptional to trade with and protect, not steal from and destroy.

Red. The color pops into my mind when I think of that rehearsal performance. Gloria Godsend—yes, the original—in crimson silk and playing the violin solo. Our U.S. Space Force Orchestra concert hall resided in the nucleus of the base, protected by missile launch pads and rooted in place by miles of twisting tunnels. Miss Godsend's soaring practice vibrato was piped into every control station and cafeteria, docked space shuttle and fighter, commercial zone condo and diplomatic spire, and everyone stopped to listen. Her solo was a special addition to Gustov Holst's *The Planets*, a movement simply called 'Andromeda.' She played perfectly, of course. There's a reason why Gloria has been replicated twenty times.

Stop thinking I'm jealous. People don't get this about clones: being together is more important to us than being unique. If your parents are test tubes and creepy-smart scientists, your bonds with the other versions of yourself become even more important. Plus, there were lessons in the lab. 'Copy without complaint' bounced off the acoustically perfect practice chambers of my childhood and cut through my mind to this day. So, the original Gloria did the solo, wore red while we wore black, played the Stradivarius while we played imitations. And that was fine with me, the second chair Gloria Godsend, the first copy. It's always fine. That woman in red transfixing all, it's really me, too, at my very best.

Crescendo—a cymbal crash—BANG! *Finis*. The orchestra rose and we bowed in perfect formation. The gold leaf and crystal chandelier, a spherical orb meant to symbolize our sun, descended and beamed sparkling amber light to every corner of the Above-the-Heavens Concert Hall. An apt name, if heaven smelled like rocket fuel and shrimp cocktail. The blinds raised on the nine half-moon windows above the top tier. I did what everyone does when they take in that view: I squinted past Earth and searched for a point half a billion miles beyond to find the tiny silver glints of Andromeda Armada starships. The creatures claim they're from a neighboring spiral galaxy, Andromeda, which Fed scientists dispute as being just too far. Wherever they came from, their dark ships blended into the black shadows of space and shimmered silver only when they were way too close, and it was far too late, for Earth to take decisive defensive military action.

Scary, but thankfully I can normally concentrate on other things. Only a few days earlier, it had been *me* who snagged black market iridescent gold eye shadow, smuggled in on a civilian transport shuttle from Earth. I'd smeared it on, and then, one-by-one, all of the twenty other Gloria Godsend violinists—including the original—came by my quarters, stuck identical manicured fingers into the liquid powder and swiped it across their identical eyelids. Rebellious, I know. "If the Andro-others want one of us, you'll be the first the Fed sends," the other Glorias warned.

Still, the cool make-up was worth it. It's not that I had wanted to be different; it's that I wanted to be the one to *decide* a few things. What was a star, except the object that shines a light on everybody, shows them what they could be, provides a perfect example of what to emulate, whether they happened to be clones or not?

The arched doors at the back of the theater retracted. The clapping died, champagne popped and fizzed, and the private-sector financial backers flowed into the gallery. The walls sealed shut again,

silencing the clink of crystal and donor chitchat.

"Xeroxed replicant dogs. Should send you back to the breeders." The maestro muttered the insults, and it was only when he turned his back to us that we knew he meant the light engineers. New equipment had been set up for the big night tomorrow and apparently a few extra flashes and scrape of cables had distracted him. The engineers were spread out, a few in the control booth, others on the catwalk, matching men with hanging heads, drooping lips and sagging eyes. Non-performers never get much attention to faces.

The maestro swept his gaze back to the orchestra. "And I must announce that music streams are cancelled. Communication security measures. That's from the top. Originals excepted, of course," he added. "They can listen in their rec room."

All twenty-one Gloria Godsends stiffened but said nothing. The five Richard Wang cellists raised a brow, the four Theodore Elstree oboists winced, and so on. Gloria edged away from me ever-so-slightly. Originals really do feel guilty when they're treated better, but apparently there's a psychological thing where they need to give the cold shoulder and be alone sometimes. On Earth, originals love their gated compounds. Still, we keep getting bred. Robots are helpful but it's easier to copy the real thing than start from scratch with computer chips and wires. Turns out clones are well-suited for prestigious careers in medicine and law, dance and music. Not to mention, when resources are scarce, certain types of people are just more useful than others. We don't ask to be bred any more than originals ask to be born. It's not our fault that the Fed decided child limits and cloning were necessary for global survival, long before arrival of the Andro-others.

"And first copies . . . you'll get directives for additional medical tests. Follow orders." The maestro's gaze rested on me for at least ten seconds. I felt my palms go slightly damp. The Fed couldn't trade us to aliens. Not really. Except, it could. The Fed was the same military-industrial complex we've had since forever. Its only evolution since the 1950s is that society now entirely accepts that corporations run the Fed and the Fed runs the world.

The maestro released us for mandatory donor schmoozing in the gallery. I went through the motions, smiling and accepting flowers, posing for pictures, making small talk, which was always about the Andromeda Armada now, the threat born from darkness. Fear and curiosity. Panic hoarding and defense prep. A guest told me that emergency directives had delayed breeding of his new racehorse.

"Sir, I'm sure the authorities will arrange a peaceful solution with the Andro-others," I murmured.

"A trade treaty, yeah." The guy nodded quickly, eying me up and down. "And then everything will go back to normal."

Normal, sure. Life with new neighbors watching over us, strange and bloodless creatures from another galaxy. They regenerate, share spinal columns that realign, nervous systems that blend. Their glowing skin membranes flatten and expand with pure oxygen. They probably float. They messaged in Morse code to imagine balloons connected with string, held in the palm of an ever-changing child, and that they are the connective tissue, they are the air that makes the balloons ascend, and they would very much like to rent a few sample Earth humans for harmless tests.

If the Fed wanted to comply, military clones were an obvious choice. Although, breeding clones isn't as easy as you might think. Partly because not everyone is willing to get cloned. Gloria had been. Everyone knew the rumors of what she had done to get ahead in the first place, decades ago, standing on a curb and watching her main competition Sonia Morales whip down a bike lane. A quick, instinctive kick of the foot, and suddenly Morales was flying headlong into oncoming traffic.

The bike tire spokes had snapped Gloria's ankle bone, the pavement scraped her elbows raw, but her fingers were unscathed. At age twenty-three they snap each Gloria clone's ankle and repair it. They even carve skin off the elbows. It's a good thing. By then, you want it to happen. It means you're good enough.

They bred more than twenty Gloria Godsend clones, I know that much. They should send a cloned dud. I was *not* expendable.

To prove my point, Above-the-Heavens Concert Hall billionaire guests, like they always do, wanted pictures of an original *together* with all of their clones. Even with the menace of alien creatures, people have their social media to think of. For a good forty-five minutes the Godsends stood in formation. As usual, I was sandwiched between the original and the next copy after me, Miss Gloria Terza. The original Gloria's rose stems jabbed me in the side.

"Sorry," she said, looking straight ahead. "I'll never get used to it."

We'd all heard those words before. Maybe an apology, or explanation, or just some tic. As usual, I checked out her dye job and whether she needed another bout of plastic surgery. Staying identical took maintenance. That would get me on a shuttle back to Earth, at least temporarily.

After the cocktail hour, the other Miss Godsends started down the tunnel back to quarters. The original, naturally, on the arm of the maestro. The others were happy to follow, Miss Terza, Miss Quarto, Miss Quinta.

Glorias 19 and 20—they were happy to be called Dici and Venti—hung back. "You all right?" They said the words simultaneously. Clones were never quite as perfect, musically speaking, copied that far from the original. However, they tended to be more intuitive.

"Just going to be alone for a while."

Dici and Venti cocked their heads. No one can be truly alone on a moon base. But they were respectful of my position of first copy, being so close to the star.

I accepted more bouquets and good-byes until the gallery emptied. The overall vibe? People felt confident that we'd put on a good show tomorrow night, convince the Andro-others that Earth humans had a lot to offer, we shouldn't be eradicated or kidnapped or whatever they had in mind. A server fetched me a last glass of champagne. I studied the white swirls of our blue planet and the stationary glare of the Andromeda ships beyond. So far, it seemed there were only two things Earth possessed that were of any value to the creatures: coffee beans and music. Turns out, nothing among the most distant stars was quite like Earth music—complex, beautiful, bursting with humor, tragedy and power.

"No music, Andro-others? None at all?" I spoke the words at the glass, wondering if they were watching me through their telescopes. Maybe they could read my perfect lips.

I left the gallery and returned to the empty auditorium. Just me and the moon dust that coated everything, no matter how many times the robotic vacuums went through. The sun chandelier glowed at the dimmest setting. Soft blue track lighting streaked up the aisles. I knew I should be resting, getting ready for the livestream performance tomorrow. Not just a livestream to Earth; a real-time show for the Andromeda emissaries, who claimed they would relay it back to Andro-buoys that comprised the transport and communications network connecting their civilization with ours. Tomorrow's live performance of *The Planets* was supposedly in exchange for scientific information on lightspeed propulsion engines.

I sucked in recycled air, strode to center stage, raised my empty arms. I commenced the maestro's newly-composed Andromeda solo. Eyes closed, I could hear every note, feel ecstasy from the audience. Midway through, I noticed Theodore Elstree slip into the chair at the end of the third row. Impossible at that distance to see which Theodore, but I knew it was Secondo, the first copy, like me. I finished to the padding of polished dress shoes on golden carpet. Theodore joined me on stage. He touched my fingers as if they were unique in the universe, touched my lips as if they could express something that had never been said before.

Long after Theodore left, I lay stretched out on stage, listening to symphonies in my mind, along with real sounds—the hum of generators, the whoosh of air conditioning, the rumble of a shuttle lift-off. If I was completely still, I felt sure I could feel the moon itself wobble slightly on its axis.

My mind flickered and spun. Any spectacle, no matter how brilliant, needs a show-stopper. An unexpected victory by the crowd-favorite underdog.

Shadows rustled in the last row and on the catwalk above. That's what I was, an underdog, although nobody, including clones, likes to be called a dog. I rose on an elbow, stared at the control booth, and beckoned the engineers closer with a wave of my hand.

The big night. Everything shone—our silk tuxedos, the theater's imported spruce wood walls and glulam columns, the star lamps projecting from each tiered box, and the sun chandelier dangling from the acoustic canopy. It illuminated our shining hands and lit the adrenaline within us to living flame that scorched pleasantly through our veins. A planetary and intra-stellar audience watched but all that really mattered was the music. I played the best I could, which is to say, I played flawlessly. In my intense concentration, I nearly forgot about my plan. But when the chandelier swung slightly on its motorized winch, throwing a different shimmering splotch of yellow onto my sheet music, of course I remembered.

The chandelier swung again, more noticeably. The conductor looked up, his face already flushing with anger, and suddenly, faster than I ever could have imagined, the half-ton light fixture plummeted. I'd done it! Well, the light engineers had done it. Something with the mechanics.

Whatever the technicalities, it helped enormously that I had anticipated this moment. Visualized it all last night. I dropped my instrument and dove to the floor, flinging my arms over my head. The original Miss Godsend reacted almost as quickly, bringing the Stradivarius to her chest, protecting it with her body. Good for her.

The crash of glass against music stands and the stage was quite deafening, and complemented by a collective scream from the audience.

The original Gloria appeared to have a head wound. Miss Gloria Quinta had the same idea as I did, and for a long second our mirror images faced off. But as the first copy, not the fifth, I simply moved faster. My elbow shoved the original Gloria and my hands closed around the undamaged Stradivarius and bow. I dodged Quinta's lunge, pivoted and crunched through crystal to front stage, as dignified anyone could be under the circumstances.

The people in the first few rows were scrambling away, but the rest of the audience stood and stared. I gazed directly at the cameras suspended from the catwalks that fed images back to Earth and the Andromeda starships.

I raised my arms high, lungs pumping for breath, glass tinkling off my black silk, slivers sticking to my skin, hair and shoulders, a lovely sparkly sheath. I had a few cuts and maybe they would become scars. So did the others. Even with the finest plastic surgeons, each of the Gloria Godsends would now be unique. But that wasn't the point. I was transformed. Radiant. Truly a star. Nobody wants perfect. People want to see the almost-perfect, the not-quite, the person *trying* to be the best. They want to see a little bit of themselves.

Believe it or not, in that moment, I knew what would happen to me next. *I'd* be cloned. Interviewed, tested, replicated. I would become an original, myself. All of my beloved clones and adoring fans, remember my words: the world will always want another superstar.

So, I commenced that solo, every note of my glorious music reaching the entire audience, human and alien, ally or enemy. After my performance, the way the applause thundered! Space is silent, but the rapture cascaded along electromagnetic waves to all those earthbound, and to those strange shipborne beings beyond.

Within the mothership, Andromeda aliens sucked espresso through their fingernails and clapped with dangling ears. Vinyl records and CDs floated in the pink-hued air and concert posters hovered on silver liquid walls.

So self-destructive, they thought at once. *And unpredictable,* they all agreed. *This is what happens when consciousness is not connected. Their souls reside in the music, and such sounds will make a marvelous leap of space and time to join the rest of the universe. Just not them.*

Slowly, the Armada backed off a billion miles, out of optimal attack range. But close enough to keep watching.

Marilee lives in Washington, DC, where she writes fiction first thing in the morning and works as a lawyer for the rest of the day. Her other stories have appeared in The Bitter Oleander, Cleaver, Metaphorosis, Orca and elsewhere. She can be found on Twitter @marilee_dahlman.

Faewild

Ephiny Gale

The following is an account of highly illegal activities related to breaches of Faewild, the realm, by Miss Emory Knight and related parties.

At the start of the beginning, Emory was sprinting towards an abandoned plot of land not far from her home. It looked like it had been an assisted living facility or halfway house before being condemned. By the time Emory was 12, the ochre and cream paint colours had faded and chipped, and all the boxy buildings were partially hidden by overgrown branches and vines.

Panting from deep in her lungs, Emory slipped through the wire fencing that blocked off the abandoned land and raced through the thicket of grasses towards the steps of the main building. The contents of her backpack jumbled and rattled as she ran.

Wilson and his friends weren't far behind: she could hear them part the fence with a metallic scrape just as she threw herself inside the main door.

[With hindsight, this had been a terribly foolish thing to do. Emory would have been much safer finding a nearby adult and seeking protection with them. Similarly, Wilson and the boys were not going to *kill* her. They might have thrown a punch where her uniform would've hidden the bruise, but all they really wanted was the contents of her bag. Surrendering would have been much more sensible, but Charlie *needed* the parcel she'd picked up from the Post Office; her parents didn't have the money for a replacement.]

She holed herself up in what looked like it could've been a storage closet, three flights of stairs up inside the main building. It was almost entirely dark, and Emory was trying to be as quiet as possible. Parts of the grasses outside had stuck to her socks. The boys were crashing about downstairs looking for her, yelling her name. The building wasn't big enough to hide her for much longer.

Desperate as a wolf in a trap, Emory reached for the only possibility she could think of: she ripped open Charlie's parcel and pulled out the jar of Portal Salve. She dipped her fingers in: the salve was black and viscous, like honey without the sugar. She smeared it across the ceiling at the back of the closet, where the roof sloped down to about head height.

With her clean hand, she reached inside the parcel again and grasped a Fae Cube, a transparent, hard plastic box a little larger than her fist. It was a little stout to properly be a cube. She gripped the box with sweaty fingers, held her breath, and then pushed through the patch of Portal Salve on the ceiling, all the way up to her wrist.

It worked. She deposited the Fae Cube on the lip of the other side of the portal and carefully retracted her hand. Then she waited as long as she dared.

[It is important to note here that opening a portal to the Faewild in an uncontrolled environment is considered reckless endangerment of the entire community, akin to committing arson in the middle of bushfire season, and Emory was exceedingly lucky that nothing life-threatening emerged from that portal during the minute or so it was open.]

The boys downstairs had got louder, like they may have ascended to the next floor. The salve on Emory's dirty hand had already begun to dry and crack, and deciding that she couldn't wait any longer, she crossed her fingers amongst the flakes so tightly that her joints hurt. Then she retrieved the Fae Cube from within the portal and felt in the darkness for the latch. Miraculously, it had flipped to horizontal, for locked. Something

was inside. Relief flooded her whole body like plunging into a hot spring; she had *caught* something.

She tore the portal from the ceiling like melted wax ripped off her mother's legs, partially so nothing else could come in, and partially so that her prize couldn't escape back out. The portal's crumpled remains were discarded to a corner of the tiny room, inert. Then she twisted the latch of the Fae Cube so its lid sprung open and its contents burst out.

The first thing she saw were the three eyes, glowing dimly milky white amongst its black backdrop. They were at roughly chin height, close enough for her to reach out and touch if she had wanted to. Then she could make out the rest of the creature, lit by the subtle radiance of its eyes: a delicate, vulpine face with six thick prehensile whiskers; two small antlers; a long body covered in grey, shimmering scales like sequins; two squat little claws at the front like a t-rex and no back legs; a shoestring tail. It was hovering in air with seemingly no effort, and gauzy clouds had started to form around its body.

Emory had never seen this variety of faewild in real life, but it was #314 in the faewild encyclopedia she'd had memorised for three years. *Fog dragon.*

The boys sounded mere meters away now. There was a protracted screech from beyond the door that could've been someone dragging a branch against a window.

"Hello," whispered Emory to her fog dragon. "I love you. Please scare them away."

She swung open the door, tongue bitten between her teeth, and the fog dragon twisted in the air towards daylight. As it flew into the hall it grew rapidly in size, so by the time it disappeared from Emory's sight its body was so wide she wouldn't have been able to wrap her arms all the way around it.

There was another final crash from the boys, some alarmed cursing, and then the screams began. They were soon replaced by heavy footfalls and a slammed front door, which then sounded like it broke from its rusted hinges and thudded to the floor like a felled tree.

Emory crept from her hiding place. The fog dragon twisted back towards her, and was shrinking again. "Thank you," said Emory. "Thank you for saving my life." It watched her with unblinking, milky eyes and continued to shrink until it could've fitted in her cupped hands, and then nestled itself in her shirt pocket, right next to her heart.

At the start of the middle, Emory was eighteen and had wrangled herself a scholarship for Sprywood College for Faewild Studies. Initially, they had hand-delivered her rejection in a gold envelope on her eighteenth birthday, making it the worst birthday of her life. Her entrance exam had been excellent, her academic marks above average, but her overall experience with faewilds officially low. Her parents had no faewilds of their own, had spent their limited extra money on Charlie's faewild ambitions, and then, even after Charlie's disappearance when Emory was fifteen, had taken too long to find the money for her to legally catch a faewild of her own at a Gateway Centre.

Unofficially, she'd been playing with, riding, and training a fog dragon for six years in secret. The fog dragon was worth substantially more than her parents' house, and if anyone saw it they would understandably ask where she'd got it, in the same tone that they'd ask why a working-class child had the keys to a top-of-the-range Porsche. Then it would have been taken away (best case) or she would've been imprisoned for how she'd acquired it (worst case), so in the end she'd mailed its Fae Cube to herself for her eighteenth birthday, to be a (not so) surprising present from a (not so) mysterious benefactor.

Then she'd ridden her fog dragon to the office window of Sprywood College's Head of Admission, feeling like real a wanker in the process, and convinced him to overturn her original rejection and add her to the very top of the waiting list. Emory's supposed ability to bond with and train a fog dragon in just a few days made her look like a prodigy. In the end, thanks to one of its existing students falling ill and dropping out, she'd only started the academic year a week later than her classmates.

It was enough to single her out. On Emory's second day at Sprywood, a freckled blonde girl slid a takeaway hot chocolate across Emory's desk before their Health & Care class, and in a soft, clear voice, asked, "So I hear you have a fog dragon?"

The girl's name was Lea. She wore polished oxfords and the kind of lush, expensive sweater that made Emory extra self-conscious about her own thrift store vest. But Lea didn't seem to care. Emory liked her immediately, the way that Emory usually liked faewilds immediately. Occasionally, during the lesson, one of them would smile at the other behind their takeaway cups. Afterwards, they compared handwritten notes, and Emory shared theories on how faewild physiology reflected the Faewild realm, and Lea brought up how human culture and health was being affected by faewilds in kind of symbiosis.

Soon, they were talking together every day. They dissected ideas for hours, and played elaborate card games, and Emory took Lea up on the fog dragon, sitting Lea in the front so she could hold onto the antlers for security. Nestled into Lea from behind, Lea smelt like mint and raspberries and sugar. From in the sky above the college, everything was beautiful.

Then they were walking with linked pinky fingers as they crossed the campus, or sitting with them entwined in their shared classrooms. Lea was conveniently left handed, so both of them still had their free hands to write with. For a while, everything was perfect--and then there was that arsehole, Sebastian Slater.

For several weeks, despite his significant popularity, both Emory and Lea were largely unaware of Sebastian's existence. Neither had noticed a pattern of Lea providing better or more detailed answers than him in class, because neither of them had noticed him at all. Sebastian, however, had certainly noticed being embarrassed and overshadowed, and his mild irritation had grown throughout the semester into a simmering rage, ultimately leading to him cornering Lea on her way back from Techniques & Training.

"Faewild fight," he spat, "9:00pm tomorrow, Court C."

Emory had wanted to alert their professors. Battling faewilds required a special license, one that none of them were eligible for until after they'd passed certain end-of-semester exams. It wasn't as catastrophic as opening up an unauthorised portal to Faewild, the realm, but it was still illegal, and Emory was already full of those kinds of secrets.

The two of them sat on Lea's bed. Lea was solemn but confident, her hands deep in the fur of her two primary faewilds, a fireshot and a phase fox. "I have to fight him, Em. If I don't do it this way, he'll find a way to hurt me or mine more directly. Hopefully, when I win, he'll leave me alone."

Emory fingered her worn leather bracelet that used to be Charlie's. Had her brother dealt with similar challenges before he vanished from Sprywood? What would he have done in their place?

The Sports Centre, and Court C, was unlocked for them: Sebastian worked there sometimes, cleaning equipment and running the occasional spin class, and had the right keys. His faewild, a chromatica, was circling Court C's court, and had literally shat inside the netball goal circle. The chromatica resembled a crow the size of a Saint Bernard, with two sets of eagle-like talons that could've cut Emory's neck in an instant. At first glance, it looked to be blind, but then you noticed that its tail fanned out like a peacock's, and that tail was covered in dozens of eyes.

Lea had brought her fireshot to the battle, slung loosely around her neck like an animated scarf. Fireshots resembled a mix of ferret, otter and opossum, a little less long than one of Lea's legs, and about as wide as her calf. Four large, solid fangs protruded like an overbite from its upper jaw. It had been kneading holes into Lea's sweater in anticipation, and a couple of blue threads had worked their way around its claws. Lea ducked her head to whisper final instructions.

Sebastian wasted little time. It began.

They were decent battlers, both of them, for teenagers who were not supposed to have battled faewilds before. But Lea was better. Sebastian had made a strategic error choosing the Sports Centre, where his chromatica could not fly for long enough to build up much speed, and where the fireshot could use the walls as leverage to launch itself at the chromatica. If they had been outside, he might have won.

As it was, the battle was a long series of attempted attacks and evasive manoeuvres, punctuated by the occasional significant hit. The fireshot ignited its back and belly mid-air and fell through the chromatica's feathered tail, burning through a third of its eyes, which fell to the shining floor in ash. The chromatica nicked the fireshot just above its hind leg, leading to an arc of blood next to the edge of the basketball court. Finally, the fireshot caught the chromatica from a blindspot and closed its fiery fangs around one of its legs, almost severing the talon clean off.

When Sebastian didn't show immediate signs of conceding, Emory stepped forward and yelled, "Enough! Put it in the cube! Do you want it to lose the claw?"

He shot her a look of utter disgust, but it seemed to break the spell. A couple of seconds later, the chromatica had retreated to the stasis of its Fae Cube. She hoped he'd bring it out later, once he had his battling license, and get it surgically seen to.

They left the Sports Centre for Sebastian to clean. Back in Lea's room, after rinsing the fireshot's wound and assessing it as relatively shallow, they applied a padded dressing and wrapped it with a bandage from Lea's first aid kit. The fireshot seemed unfazed, and made a rumbling sound Lea said was its equivalent to purring. She had caught it at a Gateway Centre when she was 10, and Emory was jealous.

They put it back in its Fae Cube overnight, just in case its health took a turn for the worst while Lea was asleep. And then Emory went back to her own room, which she regretted ever after.

Emory was woken by the chilly paws of Lea's phase fox in its incorporeal form. They had switched rooms mid-semester so that Lea's room was directly above Emory's, and often used the phase fox to pass semi-translucent messages through the floor. This time, there was no incorporeal slip of paper-- just the urgent batting of Emory's face, and then the phase fox floated over to the bedroom door, waiting for her.

Emory leapt out of bed in her worn tartan pyjamas, grabbed her mobile phone, and then hurried after the phase fox. Upstairs, Lea's door was closed. Emory yanked it open, flicked the lights: the bed was empty, the crimson bed-covers half pulled onto the floor. The phase fox flew under the bed and merged back with its solid body, which immediately started nipping at the floorboards. Emory saw them then: a small group of acid ants, each the size of one of her hands, were wandering around the room dripping acid behind them. Parts of the floor and curtains were smoking. The acid would start eating through into Emory's room before long.

She had never seen a truly wild faewild before; the domesti-spray that calmed them when they were first captured in Fae Cubes at least gave you a neutral position to start a relationship from, although of course they could grow aggressive and abdicate if you broke their trust.

A shiny spot of black poked out from behind the dishevelled bed-covers. Emory's heart dropped. With closer inspection, a rough circle of Portal Salve had been smeared on the ground beside Lea's bed, where someone might have put a water glass if they wanted to dip the sleeper's fingers in it.

Emory's thoughts swirled like a cyclone. She forced herself to breathe deeply, and then took out her phone to text her parents, plus a few friends on campus: *Faewild breach in Lea's room. Send help.*

The help would only be coming for *their* realm. No-one had ever travelled to the Faewild realm for more than a couple of minutes and returned.

Emory patted the chest pocket of her pyjamas, where the fog dragon was still curled against her chest. She grabbed the fireshot's Fae Cube out of Lea's bedside drawers for good measure, and left the phase fox to dismantle the acid ants before they caused too much damage to the building.

Then she knelt on the floor and pushed herself face-first into the dark portal. Down into Faewild.

At the start of the end, Emory climbed to her feet inside Faewild, the realm, and it was grey. After the crimson, navy and gold of Lea's bedroom, Faewild looked like someone had shifted the world's saturation dial close to monochrome. Even Faewild sun, hanging low in the sky, was a pale blonde rather than the marker-yellow or deep gold Emory remembered.

She had emerged in a patch of scrub and grasses, which was itself in the middle of an eclectic forest. A variety of pale trees were sprinkled haphazardly across the landscape, the equivalents of species that Emory didn't think would naturally grow together: pines and eucalyptus and oaks and huge succulents.

There was movement on the floor: more acid ants, dozens of them, and Emory quickly tapped her pocket to dislodge her fog dragon. The dragon grew quickly, but even as she jumped to mount it a small stream of ant acid splashed her bare toes. While the pain took a moment to register, her body immediately wanted to contort, and it took all of her willpower to get herself balanced properly on the back of the fog dragon. As they rose she allowed herself to hiss, to bury her head against the dragon's scary neck. Her left foot hung limp to one side. It still felt like it was actively burning, and the two smallest toes were simply gone.

They were barely four metres in the air when other ghostly shapes floated up from the grasses: the incorporeal forms of three wild phase foxes. They'd obviously been stalking Emory for the handfuls of seconds she'd been on the ground, and now that she was airborne they had followed in the appropriate form, clearly hoping to knock her from the sky to a position that their flesh-and-blood bodies could feast on.

"Fog," Emory snapped. "Fly."

The fog dragon shot away from the phase foxes. Emory clutched its antlers with pale knuckles, her head still tucked into its neck and her knees digging into its sides. As they flew, the frigid rush of air shocked her maimed foot and then swiftly numbed it. Soon the misty sky around them thickened to a deep fog, and the fog dragon twisted in the air and chose another direction to lose their pursuers. They switched directions twice more before the dragon slowed and Emory felt her immediate panic subside. Then it was time to find Lea.

They found her before it was completely dark. Lea's body was draped over a small hill, stomach-up and un-moving, and from the air Emory was struck with the horrific realisation that she was likely looking at a corpse. Intellectually, she had known that was the most probable outcome, but actually seeing it was a different matter.

She guided the fog dragon down at speed and the details emerged: Lea's blonde hair fanned around her head like a messy halo, already interspersed with flowering weeds like someone had deliberately woven them through. Her eyes were closed, face sallow, yellow pollen on her lips. On her left side more weeds had wrapped themselves around her fingers like rings, around her wrists like bracelets. On her right side that hand seemed to have sunk into the earth completely, and her arm was only visible from the mid-forearm up.

As she slid off, Emory realised that the same thing was true of Lea's left leg. It wasn't just bent underneath her: everything below the knee had been swallowed into the ground itself.

Emory awkwardly hobbled towards Lea, favouring her injured foot. The grief and terror overshadowed the physical pain, but walking was still tricky. She knelt and felt for a pulse, forcing herself to concentrate. Lea's neck was living-warm. The pulse was still there, if faint. Emory let out a shaky groan, and then cupped Lea's cheek, calling her name. There was no response.

Emory turned her attention to the rest of Lea. She wiped the pollen from Lea's lips with her pyjama sleeve and released Lea's hair from its entanglement. Lea's right hand was truly submerged deep in the soil. A gentle tug would not free it. In the end, Emory placed both feet on either side of Lea's right arm and pulled with all her might, and the hand finally popped out like a flower pulled out by the roots.

The hand, now freed, was dangerously red and raw, and tiny pinpricks of blood were starting to bloom across its surface where they mixed with the last bits of powdery soil. There was a clear red line across Lea's forearm demarcating which flesh had been buried. If they had been at home, Emory would have known what to do.

For now, she lay Lea's injured arm across her stomach as carefully as she could, and hoped she wasn't making things any worse.

The fog dragon had shrunk a little when they'd landed, but it had grown again and was now circling Emory and Lea, snapping its jaws defensively at unseen aggressors beyond the trees, and shrouding everything in a ten-metre radius in a low mist. Emory studied it for a moment, trying to get her breath back, and then concentrated on Lea's still-buried leg. They needed to get out of here.

But no matter how hard Emory pulled, adrenaline-filled and sweating and grunting, Lea's leg would not budge. It was like it had grown into the ground. Emory knelt in the grass and clawed at the soil around it with her fingers, which initially proved more effective, but the new parts of Lea's leg that she unearthed were a horror: bright red and shining like uncooked meat, with strong roots the size of her pinky finger impaled deep in Lea's flesh. Emory had to suppress the reflex to vomit.

She slumped in the dirt, stained and crying, while the fog dragon continued to snap its jaws nearby. Then she pulled the fireshot's Fae Cube from the deep pocket of her pyjama pants, twisted the latch, and watched the fireshot bound over to Lea's side.

"I can't free her, fireshot." Emory's voice was monotone. "But you might be able to."

The fireshot sniffed avidly around Lea, her leg, and the surrounding hill, alternately whimpering and growling, and finally stared up at Emory.

"I don't like it one bit, either, but I don't see another way we're all getting out of here."

There was a tense moment of silence broken by unnatural screeching in the trees. Emory's sweat was suddenly chilly on her skin.

The fireshot started frantically digging around Lea's leg, paws blurring, and Emory thought it may have misunderstood. But it

was simply making itself some more room. Once about six inches of Lea's leg had been re-exposed it ignited its fangs, casting the hill in fiery glow, and snapped its jaws. Everything below Lea's knee was severed instantly.

Emory hurried to check the wound, which had cauterised nicely, and thank the fireshot, whom she tucked back in its Fae Cube for safekeeping.

Lea's eyelids fluttered. Emory was thrilled to hear her name again, even if it came out raspy and weak from Lea's throat. Emory cleared the last vines from Lea's body, scooped her up as best she could, and called for the fog dragon.

They didn't go back the way they'd come. Even if they could've found where they'd entered, the chance that a portal was still open in the same place was microscopic. Instead, they simply flew through the deep dusk--it never seemed to get fully dark in Faewild--to a river where Emory hurried to clean their wounds without incident.

Once her injury had properly registered, Lea had begun to cry: the sort of strange, tearless weeping Emory might've expected from someone medically sedated. Lea said almost nothing, and in response Emory found the words pouring out of her—too many words—trying to explain and justify and apologise, and ultimately shut her mouth because she was probably just making things worse.

She felt the darkness and loss leaking out of Lea like a physical presence, and felt her own deep heart ache, and then intentionally set all of that aside until she could better concentrate on their immediate safety.

Soon after ascending again, she spotted a thin plume of smoke.

A single stream of smoke, as if released by a chimney, seemed curious enough in Faewild that it warranted investigation. Lea was still very weak, so she was propped between Emory's legs at the front of the fog dragon, and they flew with one of Emory's hands on the antlers and one around Lea's waist.

As one would expect, the smoke came from a fire, and the fire came from a cave atop a small sandstone cliff. A makeshift rope ladder had been secured around a tree and was hanging off the edge of the cliff nearby. Inside the cave appeared to be a human man.

The man had been eating some freshly-cooked spinehare meat prior to their arrival, but had frozen in place upon seeing two teenage girls riding a fog dragon, which was now hovering near the mouth of the cave.

They all stared at one another. Illuminated by the dying flames, the man's hair was longer than fashionable, shorn unevenly around his neck. Both his nose and arm looked like they'd been broken some time ago and hadn't healed quite right. His uncovered skin was covered in scars of varying shapes and sizes, as though a small child had tried to draw them on as tiger stripes, and he was missing at least three of his fingers.

When he stood and approached the fog dragon, he did so with a slight but noticeable limp. "Emory?" he asked, in a strange voice that was out of practice.

She almost lost her grip on the antler. "Charlie?"

They saved most of the conversation for the morning. Once Lea had determined it was safe to do so, she'd sunk into an exhausted slumber, and was still sleeping while Emory and Charlie spoke quietly around the ashes of the fire. Charlie's primary faewild, a zeabeer with one remaining eye, kept watch near the mouth of the cave.

It hadn't been Charlie's idea to enter Faewild. He and another classmate, Melissa Harden, had been approached by two of the richest students in his year level and offered $10,000 each if they could cross over to Faewild, the realm, for just 60 seconds. Charlie had been skipping breakfast and eating 20-cent packets of ramen noodles for dinner every day. He'd needed the money, and he'd wanted to send some back home for Emory and their parents, too. And it was only supposed to be 60 seconds.

Melissa had gone through the portal first, and then Charlie had followed her. The first 30 seconds had been tense, with glowing eyes blinking through the dark undergrowth around them, but he didn't think either of them had been hurt. Then he'd turned around and Melissa was gone--and so had the portal. He still didn't know whether something had gone terribly wrong, or whether they'd all left him there intentionally.

Emory shook her head. She'd never heard of any Melissa, and neither of those rich kids had ever said anything. "Now you can finally come home, after all, and find out."

He stared at her sadly. "I've been here for years, Emory. I don't think we're leaving."

"Maybe," she said, trying to sound more confident than she felt. "You didn't have a fog dragon before, and you didn't have me, who's memorised the percentage of faewild species that come through our nearest Gateway Centre. And now Lea and I have you, who I'd bet knows this place better than any other human alive."

She clearly had his attention. Emory took a deep breath and continued, "30% lopefoot, 25% acid ants, 20% spinehare, 15% drape heron, 10% zeabeer. Do you know that place?"

His face showed it clicking together. "That's half a day's walk away."

She beamed. "Quicker on the dragon."

The three of them climbed onto the fog dragon, Charlie behind Emory behind Lea. Wherever there was a Gateway Centre, people would be regularly opening portals in heavily controlled environments. Usually, whatever was captured in those Fae Cubes was from a subset of faewilds that naturally lived in that area, but once in a blue moon there was a notable exception.

The three of them were hoping to be that exception now.

The fog dragon wove back and forth over their target area; the equivalent of palm trees and cacti and weeping willows co-existing in Faewild's perpetual grey. Emory kissed the back of Lea's pale neck, hoping she'd hold on a little longer. They all scoured the ground for portal-sized black patches. It took some time, and some luck.

But since you're reading this, well--you know we found one.

Please be kind in your judgement.

The above statement has been declared a true and accurate account by Emory Knight (currently on remand) on the 4th day of April, 2023.

Ephiny Gale's *fiction has been published in Beneath Ceaseless Skies, Constellary Tales, and our Wyld Flash series.*

The Wyldblood 10th issue 10
Best lists

10 Best Superhero films

X2
Spider Man: No Way Home
Batman Begins
Guardians of the Galaxy
Avengers
Logan
Thor: Ragnarok
Captain America: Winter Soldier
Iron Man
Joker

And We'll Throw Your Ashes to the Wind

Emma Louise Gill

Tilly races through the open door, wide-eyed. Always in a rush, my Tilly. "Look at this, Mum!"

I smile from the corner where I'm plating dinner. "Slow down," I say, arranging fried potatoes, tomatoes and chilli. My fingers shake a little, just as they did when hand-pollinating the vegetables. Another job I'll have to teach her.

"But look." She thrusts a page beneath my nose, making me sneeze. She must have had it in her hand while running, gathering dust from the road. The fine red gets everywhere. Accentuating her beautiful curls, coating everything else in her colour, like Tilly has crept over the world.

A creature soars on the page and I blink at the blue, the grey, the water. Ocean. The script reads 'humpback whale breaching'.

"Oh." I frown. Aunty ought not to stir up the children with such things.

Setting the table, I pour half a glass of rainwater for each of us. The tank is getting low. Then I pull out Tilly's chair, and sit on mine.

Tilly bounces on her toes instead, snatching up the book. "Nate found it. He says whales are bigger'n houses." She stretches her arms out, trying to envision such size. "But Aunty says they're all dead by now."

Nate's always searching through abandoned houses for things his dad can trade. A book about the ocean isn't much use to anyone, though. I sigh.

"Aunty's right," I tell her. "Let's eat."

Her face falls, but she makes short work of the meal. She's grown tall and willowy, like her dad. Green eyes like mine, though her skin is darker. I need to wash her dress again. It's threadbare, but its long sleeves protect from the sun better than any warning I give.

She devours the pages at the table. "Are you sure? The ocean's so big you can't see the other side of it!"

My gaze flicks to the urn on its shelf. Father wanted his ashes cast out to sea from his favourite fishing spot. But rising tides eroded the cliff, and the ocean claimed it years ago. The late afternoon light catches the dust-caked silver and I can almost feel his disappointment. Reminding me to do better by my daughter. To always be honest with her.

"I used to live there," I admit.

Tilly's fork stops; she stares, open-mouthed. "What?"

I glance once again at Father. "When I was little, we lived near the beach." Memory rises: hot, grey sand, strings of cracked seaweed, windburned cheeks. "Father went line-fishing while Mother and I searched for pippis along the shore. Sometimes we chased birds, but they were too clever to catch." My tongue tastes seafood, grainy and pliable and salty. Just for a moment.

"Was there really so much water you could dunk your whole body in?"

I smile. "Yes, though you'd come out crusty." Tilly frowns. Rubbing my dusty arms, I try to resist scratching the bloody patches on my neck. I ought to get them checked. "Seawater is different to rain. Lots of salt. And later, poison." Runoff from a dead land.

Rust-red flecks mar my glass. I wipe them away with a fingertip. "You couldn't drink it either, not till it had been through a factory to remove the salt." Back then, the government still claimed the climate would improve. That the change was temporary.

My drink is stale, while my memories are uncomfortably fresh. "Anyway, the sea rose, flooded the coast, and broke the factories. You know the story. We came here."

Tilly snatches her hand from her glass, as if afraid its contents will swallow her too.

Resurfacing from those days, I struggle to give her another smile. "Your dad helped set up the cloud seeder drones, you know, to try to get more rain to fall."

She nods, but vaguely. She never met him, doesn't carry the undying weight of her father like I do mine.

"Did he live by the ocean too?" she asks.

"No. He was a farmer." Until the drought killed that too. Trapped between salt and sun.

I finish my water, gesture for her to do the same. Gather up the dishes to scrub. "Put the book away, honey."

"Why?" A teenager's challenge.

Because you shouldn't wish for something you can't have, I want to say.

Father's urn watches me. Does his last wish matter, when the rest of his life was full of unanswered ones?

"No one visits the ocean anymore," I say. "There's nothing there for us."

Tilly wants to go, of course.
"For history's sake," she says.
"For my birthday," she pleads.
"Because I want to," she tantrums.
In the end, I can't say no. Either that, or she'll try to go with Nate anyway.

We are a small community: news spreads fast. Nate's dad finds a way to keep him home, so it's just Tilly and I who head out with bikes, a trolley, and three days' supplies. I've a list of items people need, if we can find them. We travel north along the old highway, then west in the afternoon. Tilly barely complains. My legs aren't used to the exercise, and the seat sores are going to be awful. But when I look at her, cycling ahead with the wind in her hair, framed by acacias and the black-brown landscape, I know I would do anything for her.

My own mother's sunken face flashes in my mind. I wobble; the trolley tips over. I stare at it lying in the dust.

She abandoned us years ago. 'Wandered off to feed the wildlife,' as they say. I can't stop thinking about her since Doc asked for meds yesterday. He thinks we should try the old pharmacies, where safes might be rusty and breakable by now. I doubt there'll be anything worth taking, but I'll look nonetheless. It's the least I can do, after he used the last best drugs for my father.

And now I really think about it, Mother took a lot too.

I right the trolley and bike, wincing at my pounding headache. I feel older than I should. Tilly brings over water but I refuse hers and sip my own. The patches on my neck itch like hell today. Doc said he needs to see them when I get back. His tone was weird. Like Mother's before she left.

"You know I'll always stay with you," I promise Tilly.

She gives me a look. "Mum."

"What?" I smile. "It's true."

"Let's just go," she says.

At the edge of the crumbling city is a collection of old shops. I help Tilly through the shards of a front window, its empty facade framed by peeling orange paint. A broken mannequin sits like a guard. Someone once lit a cigarette in her hand and left it to burn. The other places we investigate are not much better.

"Let's make this a game," I suggest. We search for supplies in the dim and dust, awarding pretend points. We laugh at old kids' magazines, wonder at strange appliances with no purpose—or power. The trolley gains a ripped tarp; three cans of dried chickpeas; a pair of binoculars with a cracked lens. I find a blue cap in an office, its embroidered yellow Eagle still bright. Tilly puts it on, giggles, and pretends to fly, zooming in and out of the growing shadows.

I don't tell her those birds make me shiver. About the time I saw raptors eating a drowned corpse. She needs her childhood.

The shore, when we find it, is kilometres further inland than I remember. It creeps in around white-painted walls and the crumbling bricks of old houses, a whispering that becomes an overwhelming presence. The lapping water echoes, a slow hush of incoming waves, curling into a soft crash, before racing out again. High tide mars the buildings, stained and dirt-streaked. My nose wrinkles against the salt and water-logged decay.

The road is too rough for our bikes, so we leave them inside a bus shelter littered with animal droppings and bones. It is nearly dusk.

Tilly kicks stones into the water and complains this isn't what she thought it would be like.

She is the one to find the whale skeleton, a bone-white monument in the mud of an old, drowned football field. Its ribs make arches that she darts between like the scavengers who stripped it clean. I stand in its shadow and wonder what drove the creature to this. Whether it knew its end had come.

Tilly's arms stretch out. "It's as big as our house." We stare at the whale, quiet for a moment. "Aunty was right, wasn't she," she says.

I wish she hadn't been.

Tilly scrapes desiccated barnacles off the bones. They shine almost brighter in the orange sunset.

We return to our bikes, and sleep snuggled together for the first time in years. I don't know if it's the coolness of the night, or the presence of the sea, but Tilly is quieter than usual, more thoughtful.

"Where'd all the people go, Mum?" she asks. "Are there ghosts here?"

I hold her tight. "Probably. But I'll never let them hurt you."

The stars fade into lilac dawn.

"Happy birthday to me!" yells my daughter to the startled crows. We eat chickpeas for breakfast, though Tilly insists on no more than thirteen, since that's her age now. We laugh together, and I give her the perfume I found yesterday, a miniature bottle that had escaped looters. It's called 'Ocean Breeze.'

She sniffs it. "Not very accurate, I know," I say.

"No. But I like it," she replies.

We return to the whale, then another kilometre and up a small hill. There it is: the sea. A sparkling, white-capped expanse stretching to the horizon. Tilly runs past me, down to the water, screaming in joy. A seabird calls and she caws back at it. Digs her toes into the silt at its edge.

"Don't go in," I remind Tilly, because it is a strange purplish colour, not blue like Nate's book. Foaming algal mats float near the shore. Pollution and years of drowned civilisation will have added to the toxicity.

It's a blustery day. The First People call this season Bunuru, Second Summer, though now the heat extends to April. I kneel on the grey, muddy ground and say thank you to the earth the way Aunty taught me, making myself known to Country. Then I try to find shade, hiding from the sun. A greater threat than the water.

Tilly's bright curls stick out under her new hat. Waves lick the ground, devouring it piece by piece. My father's urn is heavy in my backpack.

I think of him, how his generation lamented the past, held onto it so hard it seemed more real than the present. I think of the work he did, keeping us alive. Of the time Mother and I filled our pippi bucket and he caught three fish and we had a feast. Of the smile I missed, after Mother died. His silence after Tilly's dad proposed, and after he left to set up drones in other towns and never returned. Father only said I had to take care of my baby above all else.

I take out his ashes. It's not his fishing spot, but "We're here," I whisper. "Hope this is okay."

Tilly joins me at the water's edge, breeze blowing offshore. Clouds pass over the sun.

"Do you think it might rain?" Tilly asks, excitement in her eyes. She's only tasted it twice.

"I hope so," I say. "What do you think of the ocean?"

She shrugs. "It's okay. But not really for us." She holds my hand. "Thanks for bringing me anyway, Mum."

My eyes sting in gratitude for the beautiful person she is becoming. I release the ashes to the wind, to the sea.

"Goodbye," we say. Tilly sprays Ocean Breeze into the wind after him.

We turn for home.

Emma Louise Gill (she/her) is a British-Australian speculative fiction writer, coffee lover, and cat herder. Her short stories appear in AntipodeanSF, Etherea Magazine, and forthcoming in Where The Weird Things Are (Deadset Press, 2022), among others. She narrates for AntipodeanSF Radio, blogs at www.emmalouisegill.com, and procrastinates on Twitter @emmagillwriter.

Love in the Apocalypse:

A Soldered Epitaph

M.A. Dosser

Tuck pried another sheet of aluminum from the wall. With his soldering gun, he marked, "Brenna Wallace. Wife, Sister, and a better Mother than I deserved."

Those few words were all that Tuck could manage before he carefully placed the plate inside the airlock with the others.

He paused. He could join them, could open the hatch now, without his space suit.

Brenna. Max. Rosie. Milo. The names stared at him.

Crying, he went inside then flipped the switch, letting their tombstones drift out of the space station.

Tuck watched as his family began their orbit around the scorched Earth.

A Fire Before Dawn

Paul Alex Gray

I walk behind you through the woods, slipping between trees as quiet as a ghost. I move carefully, trying not to get too close, even though I know you won't see me. You're dead. Of that I'm certain, yet I can't help but follow you.

This is not a good place. It is not a real place either. I don't know if it's something spawned in my mind. A vision?

It is a nightmare of our childhood.

Not long ago these woods were bright and green and graced with songbirds that would call at dusk, in cascades of lilting notes. Now the bark is brittle and dry. It crumbles into dust, should I touch it. The only sound is the whispering of dead leaves.

Pieces of our lives are scattered here and there. Moments from before, when we wandered these woods as boys, laughing and joking. Chipped ceramic bowls and upturned chairs. A soccer ball, and filthy clothes, fabric caked with dirt and locked in broken poses. I pick at a crayon in the earth, deep red and cracked. I think our mother bought it for us.

The beast slinks by, a shadow ash grey. It moves through the trees to our left, skulking low, open-mouthed and brazen. Its gaze fixed on you.

47

I shout at it, clap my hands, and it turns to face me, sharp teeth cut like stones, breath steaming. It's eyes flash, amber coins, minted from hate.

There's a thudding noise far away and the trees shudder. A roar begins to tear the sky, the rumble of jets.

Just as you did that day, you begin to run.

Your son fits in here. He has grown so much, the years have made him big and strong.

There are daytime moments when I think I perhaps I can fit into this place too. Where maybe… I can be something more than broken.

This morning I am lacing up his skates. Carefully I pull and loop, tugging them tight. I wipe the shining blades and place his feet down.

He looks just like you. Dark eyes, as deep as forever. The coach calls the boys and he marches out with his team. He is red and black and white striped. He soars on the ice as a bird flies.

Even here, the beast lurks, although none but I can sense it. At this moment, it sits by a man who stands and sits and stands in his seat, watching his own son play. He pays no attention to the beast. He doesn't smell its acrid stench, cannot see its jagged teeth.

It's thinner than it once was. Hungry, perhaps.

As I sit alone, stomping my feet in the cold and looking out at the white rink below, I listen to it breathing.

Sometimes it moves to the rink glass, padding unseen between the parents and siblings that have come to watch the game. It opens its great maw, its breath clouding the glass.

I've learned to stay quiet. It's better that I don't shout out in public.

If I stare at it long enough, it will turn to face me.

I am older now than you were when I lost you. This puzzles me endlessly.

Your wife calls me a man now. She says my bravery saved your son and saved her too. Helped us come to this place, to safety and to a future. She tells me you would be proud.

I've never told her about the beast. How it followed us here. That it stalks me everywhere I go. That it has been looking at your son.

Sometimes I walk to the park after work. I have found secret pathways only visible when I'm alone. Little trails that lead through the woods, under the highway and out past the fields. They take me to the bad place. They take me back to you.

Sometimes there are others from before. Do you remember the old man who sold figs from his cart? This past summer I found him. He was standing still, his tired shoulders slumped forward. I asked if he had seen you, but he shook his head nervously.

I asked him for some figs, but he cursed and stamped away.

Once I saw an old woman who may have been our grandmother, although I barely remember her now. It was winter and the lands between us were painted white. The trees glittered and spoke with the sound of a fire dying.

She was walking by a snow-covered road, singing songs I thought I'd forgotten. Lights flashed, and a car zoomed by and she was gone.

Tonight, the wind howls with the rage of a storm coming. Leaves of gold and red spin circles across the empty streets.

"There's a wolf outside."

My skin crawls and I stare in shock.

"What did you say?" I ask.

Your son is wearing Spider-Man pyjamas, bouncing on the couch and staring out the window.

"I saw a wolf. Out there, by the streetlight."

"No, darling," says your wife. "There are no wolves here. It must be a dog."

"It was a wolf," he says. "Uncle, it really was."

"I'll go take a look," I say, worried they'll hear the tremor in my voice.

I leave without my jacket, running down the stairs of the apartment complex. The wind bites with a cold that cuts through my clothes. Sleet skitters across the street in great tendrils.

Up ahead, I see a shadow slink away, and I chase. I am more furious than afraid.

This is the first time that your son has seen it.

"Get away!" I shout in a voice cracked and trembling. "You shouldn't come here!"

The beast turns, bright eyes reflecting the streetlights. It's impossibly large now, but its skin hangs loose on gaunt bones. Its mouth hangs open, its filthy tongue limp. It hobbles off, heading to the pathways. To the woods. It's coming for you.

I run, moving across the crunching leaves, following the secret pathways. I can smell the smoke, closer this time. The sky beyond the woods is tinted orange, glowing in the clouds. I hear jets rumbling, coursing through the night. My heart pounds as I pursue the beast. My hands shake and I feel sick, but I am driven now, filled with rage.

And then, I see you. Scrambling through the woods, frantic with fear. I cry out, wishing I could go to you and hold you, take your hand and tell you it will be alright.

"I'm here!" I shout, but of course you don't hear me.

You never do.

I tumble over splintered wood and broken plates. Pieces of our home crunch beneath my feet. Voices spill around us, words dull as if spoken through mouthfuls of dirt and ash. I force my head up, not wanting to look down. I'm sure there are faces there, the dead whispering fearful and hateful things.

The beast howls, almost upon you.

"Stop!" I shriek.

And then I am holding your son, but he's a baby again, just as I had done when you gave him to me all those years ago, when we had to escape. A tiny bundle of light wrapped in rags. You told me to hide and pushed us away before you ran, shouting to draw the attention of those that sought us.

Now, as he did then, your son squeals and wriggles in my arms. In the distance, jets tear the sky ragged.

The beast stands silhouetted by fire and smoke. Towering before us, teeth flashing, jaws wide like it intends to swallow us whole. Its tongue is long and rough, slick and poisonous.

"Leave us alone!" I shriek.

Its great maw widens, lips drawn back over jagged yellow teeth in a mockery of a smile. It pads toward us, eyeing your son.

Then your voice comes, from a time before.

Run.

The ground trembles and shakes.

"No!" I shout.

I won't let it take your son. I'm running, but not away. Not this time. I dash toward the beast. Its eyes widen, and I crash into it. I feel its fur, sense its weight sliding beneath, jaws snapping and spit flying. With one arm, I grab at the beast's head, clawing at its eyes. In my other arm, I hold your son tight.

All together we are falling, tumbling, our bodies wrapping together. Flesh and fur and fear. We twist and spin as the trees around us crash and splinter, folding in, branches breaking as smoke and noise and ash swallow the world.

It is your son's tenth birthday today.

I sit in my bedroom, watching bleary eyed as the sky bleeds into light. I have his gift in my hands. New skates, blades sharpened and gleaming, wrapped in red paper with a bow.

The beast is here, sleeping on the floor beside me, breathing deeply. Its fur is threadbare and caked with dirt. Dried blood crusts its feet. How long has it been running?

How long have we been running?

I have been awake all night trying to remember the sound of your voice. I feel that I've forgotten it. That the memory is just my mind imagining how you sounded.

My eyes hurt and I feel I have no more tears to cry.

I remember how we would play before bedtime, joking and laughing. When you slept, you breathed so loud and slow and I used to think that sound had been what carried me away to dream.

I hear noises in the kitchen. Your wife is making a special breakfast. I open the door and stand in the hall.

"I won't let you take him," I say to the beast.

It opens its eyes, the whites flecked with blood. I wait for it to answer. It stares at me for a moment and then glances away. I turn and look out my window. Big fat snowflakes are falling. The wind has stopped, and the whole world is painted white and new.

The sound of footsteps shakes the floor and I turn to see your son running down the hall. He leaps to hug me, clutches me tight, his eyes bright. I look at the beast and then back to him. He follows my gaze, but simply smiles and hugs me. He does not see it.

"Uncle, why are you shaking?" he asks. "What's wrong?"

The beast lowers its head and closes its eyes. I try to take a breath without shaking.

"I'm excited," I say, tickling your son, moving down the hall. "It's your birthday! I'm happy for you. Come, I have something for you."

There was a morning before it all began. When we were young. Maybe you remember? It was midsummer, when the frogs croaked in the stream behind our house. You woke me from my bed and took me outside.

You led me through the field and into the trees. I shivered, rubbing sleep from my eyes. It was dark, but I knew it was not night. I was scared, and I asked you if wild beasts lived in the woods. You told me not to be silly, but you winked, and held my hand anyway.

We ate some figs and you smoked one of grandpa's cigarettes. You took me to the pond where the birds would bathe on hot days. At that moment, just before dawn, the water was perfectly still. It reflected the brightening sky, a whole other world I never knew was visible.

There were only a few stars left. I asked you where they went in the daytime. You laughed and smoked and told me that the stars were always there, but I did not believe you.

Then you gave me a pebble. You told me you would teach me a magic trick.

You helped me curl my arm back, and together we threw the pebble out into the pond. When it fell, the water seemed to reach up and swallow the stone like some giant fish gulping a fly.

I watched the ripples flowing, and I wondered if they would echo forever.

Paul Alex Gray writes linear and interactive fiction starring sentient black holes, wayward sea monsters, curious AIs and more. His work has been published in Nature Futures, Andromeda Spaceways, PodCastle and others. Chat with him on Twitter @paulalexgray or visit www.paulalexgray.com

Atop Dead Trees

Elizabeth Broadbent

Killian slumped in a plastic hospital chair, head lolled against a white wall. Needles tugged my arms as I scrambled upright. Why was I hooked to IVs? Why was my high school boyfriend there? I'd been buying a latte. I'd smelled espresso. Machines beeped around me as a small, frightened sob slipped out.

Killian wrapped around me before I could speak. "Shhh, Lila. You—"

Weakly, I wiggled from his arms. "Where's Bruce?"

"Who?" His eyebrows met. "Baby, someone ran a red and hit you while you were jogging. You've been out for three days."

My throat tightened. I scrunched up under the rough-woven blanket. "This isn't funny. Get Bruce."

"Who?" He reached for me again.

I ducked. "My husband. Where is he?"

"I think we need your doctors." Killian's chin-length hair brushed my shoulder. He smelled so familiar. I could've closed my eyes and slipped back into my teenage years. "I'll sit here, okay?"

I pulled away. "Where is my *husband*?"

"Shhh, honey."

"We *broke up*. I went to Berkeley and—"

Killian's mouth tightened, but his voice stayed calm. "Honey, we went to UVA. We got married right after graduation." Careful not to disturb the needle, he lifted my left hand. "See? The doctors wanted to take it off while you were here. I wouldn't let them."

I wore a sapphire engagement ring.

Bruce had given me a diamond.

I slammed back. I wasn't dreaming— dreams didn't hurt and IVs ripped at my arms. I screamed. Killian shushed me as nurses rushed in. "He's not my husband!" I shouted, smacking him away. Needles tore

and I screamed again. "We're not married! Get Bruce! Bruce E—"

A shot in my thigh. Black spots hazed together, then I was blinking at a white ceiling.

"Hey, honey." Killian stroked my forehead. "You hit your head pretty hard. They want to run more tests. But they're thinking you have temporary amnesia."

Get Bruce, I wanted to yell. But that sapphire—had I imagined everything? Bruce, my friends, my yellow kitchen, my whole *life*?

No. I'd waited in a Starbucks line. I'd smelled of coffee beans instead of antiseptic; an espresso machine had whirred.

"So where—where are we?" My voice teetered.

"Richmond. St. Mary's." He combed his fingers through my greasy, unwashed hair. "We live in my parents' house. They passed. So have yours. We took over their bookstore. No kids, no pets." He smiled a bit. "No days off, really."

My parents were dead. I hadn't escaped to San Francisco. I lived in Richmond with my prom date.

They ran tests. I stayed numbed, quiet. I'd dropped into someone else's life. Endlessly patient with what they called my "memory lapses," Killian never left. At my discharge, he handed me a scrap of cloth. "I brought your favorite mask."

I must have looked blank.

"The pandemic?" Gently, Killian slipped the covering onto my face and tightened it, then slid on his own.

My stomach flipped. "Does it kill you?"

"Only if—" He sighed. "No. Yes. Not you, okay? You're vaxxed. You'd feel like you had a bad cold, probably."

St. Mary's had a monorail station, but we walked the wrong way. Instead, Killian led me to a dimly lit building. I stared. "What's this?"

He glanced at me. "What?"

"This building. It's full of cars."

He took a moment before answering. "It's a parking deck, baby."

"There are so many cars they have a *building*?"

"Lots of people come to the hospital," Killian replied, but his eyes slid sideways, like a parking deck was something important, like not recognizing it meant something more than not recognizing him.

I couldn't figure out how to strap myself in. Killian helped. As we turned onto the road, a terrible smell slammed me. "This runs on *gas*?"

Killian reddened. "We can only afford part-electric. The bookstore—"

"What about the climate?" I asked.

"Oh, baby. I know how guilty you feel about using gas. But one electric car wouldn't have saved the polar bears."

I stared. "The polar bears are dead?"

Killian went quiet. Finally, he said, "There are some in zoos."

When I began to cry, he picked up my hand. Cars clogged the streets like plaque in a sick man's arteries.

While he cooked dinner, I hunted for a holoscreen, then turned on an old TV. There'd been "another" mass shooting. Killian found me crying again.

"Lila?" His voice rose. "What happened?"

"Are we at war?"

He hesitated. "No. I mean yeah, we're always at war, but—"

"Then why do people have guns?"

He sank down and held me.

Killian had grilled meat. We had an enormous lawn but no solar panels. On a handheld computer, *The New York Times* told me that Beijing couldn't breathe and whales wouldn't stop beaching themselves. Killian mentioned the president, elected for a second, non-consecutive term. Bruce and I had always hated his TV show. Bruce. Killian rubbed my back while I wept. "This isn't my life," I managed.

He lay down and curled around me. "This'll pass."

"What if it doesn't?"

Killian took a long time to answer. "Then we figure it out. We always have."

He must have held me until I slept. Whenever I woke, his knees were tucked behind mine, and we breathed together.

"You'll be okay while I'm at the bookstore?" Killian asked in the morning. His lips brushed my cheek.

I had decided, in the night's dark and quiet, that I would leave. He wouldn't find me—I'd give him that grace. But I'd read words they used to describe their slow-moving catastrophe: climate refugee, police brutality, smog.

Killian's eyes were kind. He seemed so worried. "Honey, I don't like leaving you alone."

I could walk away from it, or I could take a gift offered amid so much sadness. Maybe that sadness made it more precious.

"Lila? Do you want to come with me?"

I stood. The wooden floor felt smooth, cool under my bare feet. Atop those dead trees, I slipped my hand into his.

Elizabeth Broadbent has published speculative prose poetry in Bewildering Stories, Down in the Dirt, and AntipodeanSF (forthcoming). She lives in the United States with her three children and husband.

Freely Given

Connor Mellegers

Forty ravs on the Bone and it was all the Tech could talk about. Taye did it, so said everyone. His name was on the lips of every student at the Tech the same as if he'd given the money straight to them. Forty ravs. Enough to live on for years if you were careful, and he'd given the lot to the Bone as if it were nothing. Sheena said Taye had shown her the scars he'd got on his hands and knees working to earn it through all sorts of hard labor. And now the secret was out, and students and instructors alike were lining up to shower him with praise, and affection, and gifts of their own. Already, stories of the gifts he'd received were spreading like wildfire, fueled by the fact that he made a grand display of denying that he had donated anything at all. Genuine humility of course. Someone like Taye would never aggrandize. After all, he'd given forty ravs to the Bone.

I met Joan in the gymnasium of the Three Oaks community center. The huge wooden room was empty save a few stray balls and frayed mats scattered across the floor. Normally, the entire gym would be covered in after-school activity refuse: pylons, hoops, balls of all shapes and sizes, but all of those were neatly away in the storage room, which meant Joan had got a serious head start on me. I rushed to the supply closet and grabbed a push-broom. By the time I got back, Joan had put everything away and had already begun disinfecting the equipment. I put my head down and began sweeping.

Joan and I had been assisting the center managers for years. They were responsible for the center's operation of course, but between managing their programs and

53

supporting the needs of their visitors they barely had any time to keep the facility clean. We provided our labor as a gift to the managers, and they kept the center running as a gift to the entire community. After our labor, we would record our gifts in the official registry. Both of us checked off what we had each done of the sweeping, mopping, sanitizing, etc. What work each of us did impacted how much official credit we would receive and thereby the gifts, respect, and esteem that would follow in equal measure. Unofficially, what we did affected how the center's managers saw us. You could see them following your pencil as you marked off what you'd done, raising their eyebrows in appreciation, or letting them furrow in disappointment. You could hear it in their voice too. "Thank you for your generous gift to Three Oaks *AND* thank you for *yours*." It was all in that *and*. I couldn't be that *and*. Not today. Not after Taye had given forty ravs to the Bone.

Joan started mopping the second I'd swept up the dust and dirt. I nearly ran to fill another bucket and begin mopping from the opposite side. I kept my head down, my motions fluid and perfect. Mopping half a gym may only have been worth half the credit, but if I was quick enough, I could get to the next task before Joan and have a chance to catch up to her. After five minutes mopping in silence, I finally turned to look at her from across the room. She was grinning.

"What?" I said, turning my eyes back to the floor, desperate for this chance to clean while she was distracted.

"You heard about Taye," she said. I groaned and she laughed. Of course. She knew exactly why I hadn't taken a breath since I arrived. She'd been laughing at me the whole time.

"Everyone heard," I said. "Very generous of him to give all that money. Thirty ravs was it?"

Her smirk made my stomach jump. "Forty. And you don't have to rush, you know. I'll split credit with you, whatever we've done."

I mulled it over. It was clever of her, but that was no surprise coming from Joan. Splitting credit meant that officially we'd done the same work and would share whatever esteem we'd earned in the eyes of the community. Considering what she'd already done, that was a generous gift, though a gift to one person was nothing compared to a gift to the entire community. I could refuse, of course, but that would be disrespectful. Perhaps doubly so for the base intentions with which the gift would have been received.

"Oh please, Ev, I won't tell anyone," she said.

Another gift, this time hidden. At this point, refusing would be irresponsible.

"Thank you," I said.

"Taye won't get official credit without disclosing openly," Joan said.

"And that just makes it more impressive."

She nodded and scrubbed at a stubborn spot on the floor. Anonymous gifts were often the most worthy. Little chance of credit meant that a gift could truly be freely given. But they were rare. A gift-giver deserved their credit and had a right to it. Earning official credit meant that everyone could see what you'd done. The higher your credit, the greater gifts you would receive from those around you. Everyone wanted to give to the most generous and share in the righteousness of their generosity. But Taye had given a massive gift in near-perfect silence. And he'd given to the Bone. Few ever gave to the Bone and what little they did was rarely worth having. Anyone could take from the Bone, whatever they wanted and however much they wanted. A crowd of takers, ingrates, and even hoarders could enter that sad little building on the edge of town and walk off with all forty ravs without so much as a reason. Few had it in their hearts to give to those who took from the bone. To give cash was even more unheard of.

But Taye hadn't cared. He must have labored for wages for months – hard, thankless work without any credit or respect – just to anonymously dump it all directly to the Bone. And his gift would never appear on the official ledgers or records. Those takers and hoarders would never know who had given them all that money. A gift like that was unheard of. But we did hear of it. And now, official credit or not, everyone knew what he had done. It was genius. Genius and risky. Hell, who wouldn't be impressed? Even I'd go out with Taye if he asked me, not that I was looker enough to be asked. If he did, it would just be another gift to his credit.

"It is *very* impressive," Joan agreed. The edges of her curly black hair bobbed into the soapy water as she bent over the bucket. "But it's hard to believe Taye could earn that much money through labor alone."

"Sheena saw the scars," I reminded her.

She scoffed. "Everyone has scars, they don't mean anything just because a credit-hungry looker like Sheena thinks they do. Any labor worth doing is given as a gift. Earning wages like that means taking on labor no one else wants to do, work in a factory or mine, or some other horrible place. Taye's a shrimp from a good family. Wage labor enough to earn forty ravs would break him." She snapped up and her eyes landed on mine. "Unless he had help. Or maybe it was a gift. Maybe he wasn't the one who made the donation at all."

My mouth dropped and my feet squeaked on the gym floor. A gift gifted. Credit for an incredibly generous donation freely given away. That wouldn't just be impressive, that would be astronomical. Untouchable. Worth all the respect you could imagine. Even without official credit, if that leaked, you'd have more than just half the Tech longing for you. Hell, even the instructors might go for you.

"You heard something?" I asked.

"No, I didn't hear anything," she said.

I huffed and slammed my mop into the bucket, splashing water all around me.

"Then why even bring it up?" It was hurtful to get my hopes up like that. That kind of gift would be fantastic to witness. To even be in the presence of that kind of generosity is something everyone dreams of.

Joan sighed one of her big sighs. Older sister sighs, I call them, even though we're not related and my mom sometimes makes gifts of meals to her family. All the more significant for the fact her family isn't offered many gifts.

"What I mean, Ev, is no one has heard anything, *yet*. But maybe they could. And who knows what name could be attached. I mean, there's no official record, anyone could have done it."

I stared at her for a long time. Joan wasn't a looker, same as me. She wasn't particularly athletic either. Her math and writing weren't enviable and no student at the Tech would want to trade places with her in a million years. But she had these ideas sometimes. Wild ideas. Ideas so twisted it hurt my brain to try and wrap itself around them.

"Anyone could have done it," I said, my mouth still failing to close.

"Anyone," she agreed.

"Like you?" I asked.

"Oh no," she shook her head in big arcs. "Who would believe that? My family are known takers," she said.

I nodded and turned away. We never talked about it. It felt shameful to even mention. Her parents accepted any gifts they were offered and even took from the Bone: money, food, furniture, whatever they needed. But they never gave to anyone. They never seemed to labor at all. True takers. And Joan carried the stain of their greed. No one would believe she was capable of such generosity.

"But you could have done it," she said.

I scoffed. I wish I'd done it. I wish I could have done it. I'd never had anywhere near forty ravs in my life. I only ever labored as a gift. I never needed to work for anything so shameful as pay.

"Your grandmother visited last year, didn't she? I heard she was a hoarder."

I tried to scoff again but my tongue was dry and heavy. Joan was really saying this. Grandma Ross was a hoarder and a wage taker. It had always brought my dad shame, but he still invited her to stay with us every year. Hoarders sometimes gifted chunks of their fortune to family members. It was known to happen. It might be believed. But to really suggest taking credit for someone else's gift? I'd never even heard it done before. A credit thief would be below even the least remorseful takers.

"Joan, we couldn't..."

"Couldn't what? Tell people what we might have heard?" She laughed, picked up her mop and bucket, and left the gym, leaving me behind to stare. She didn't look back.

Billy was the first. Then Eliza-Beth. The king and queen of lookers at the Tech. Then the rest followed: Cara, Saraisa, Johanssen, Themi, all the lookers worth seeing lined up outside my locker between classes. And the instructors. The grins they gave me when I passed by could light up a room. Huge, massive things that made you feel like the smartest kid in the Tech. And suddenly I was, however you sliced it. My grades went through the roof. Study notes from lectures I'd never heard and essays I didn't remember writing popped up in my bag and my locker, gifts from instructors and students alike, freely given and taken. And yet, even accepting them, my collateral didn't drop. It couldn't. My gift had been that big, that selfless, that colossally unheard of. A donation that large and the credit for it freely given away. I could take jobs for wages. I could take gifts from anyone who offered. I could be the biggest hoarder there ever was

and I'd still be the greatest gift giver the Tech had ever seen. I was infallible.

One day my dad called me in after school. He's a big man, tall and grim. He has a massive smile, the kind like Eliza-Beth's that could light up a room with only the flash of a few teeth. But we never saw it at home. He always said his smiles were gifts and they were too precious to waste on family. But that day he smiled. Mom too. Even Geoffrey, who'd never given or accepted anything from me a day in his life was smiling. They all had gifts in their hands. Delicately wrapped in the paper and ribbons you saved for really special occasions. I smiled back at them.

"Here are some small tokens of our appreciation," my father said. Small tokens. He *ACTUALLY* said that! My father had met mayors he was less respectful to, lifelong dedicants and gift-givers of the highest order who didn't hear such words, but he said them to *me*.

Of course, not all those who looked were lookers. I once saw Taye from across the Tech cafeteria. His stock had fallen dramatically after everyone found out it was me who had given 40 ravs to the bone and not him. Everyone knew I had given him the credit freely. But even freely given, accepting credit for another's donation is pathetic. Pathetic to the highest order.

I was surrounded by people as always. They jostled to see who would be able to gift me lunch. They pressed around me, beautiful meals made with love offered up with admiration and desperation. Whatever lunch I accepted bathed the giver in the light of my generosity, earning them the highest credit possible from one small gift. I took one, a dal made by a looker named Kiel. It smelled amazing. The others pulled back, staring crestfallen at their unaccepted lunches.

Across the cafeteria, Taye pulled out a brown paper bag lunch. Eating one's own lunch was something only takers and those most pathetic were ever forced to do. No one cooked for themselves by choice. Back before my star had risen, I would sometimes swap what I had made with someone else. It wasn't prestigious but at least our meals were gifted.

I thought of asking one of those I'd rejected to give their lunch to Taye as a gift to me. But then I saw him slide his bag across the table as someone else did the same. I couldn't make out who it was before Kiel pulled me to their table and into that afternoon's gifts.

I was laying on the hill outside of the Tech with Billy and Eliza-Beth. We were drunk and sweet off compliments and the summer air and all sorts of gifts freely given and taken and given back in return. Joan walked up the hill to greet us. We were covered only by a thin, white blanket. She smiled and the three of us giggled. Joan was from a family of known takers. Even a giggle was a gift.

"Enjoying your afternoon?" Joan asked. I hadn't seen her in ages. Our work at Three Oaks was a thing of the past, just as needing to labor for credit was a thing of the past. The three of us stared at her, smiling and unblinking.

"It's funny," Joan said in her older sister tone. "How much a gift can change your life. Receive the right gift and you might find yourself surrounded by friends you never even knew you had."

Billy barked a laugh. "And what would you know about giving gifts?" he asked.

"I know that accepting them can cost just as much as giving them," Joan said.

Billy and Eliza-Beth both laughed maniacally and rolled into each other, pulling me back into a pile of kisses. They both joked, as we rolled around, about the taker who thought she could educate us on gifts.

I tried to let the sun and grass and attention wash over me, but Joan's words flew around my mind long after she'd left our private hill. I had forgotten. In the face of the gifts, and attention, and love that felt so right, so perfectly right, I had forgotten where they came from. I had let myself believe that this was my life, finally earned after years of under-acknowledged labor, creativity, and kindness freely given to those around me. But in reality, it had been a gift, one bestowed on me by Joan through the rumors she'd spread.

It is not a bad thing to accept a gift. But to take more than you give, to think only of what you can take, that is what makes a taker. When I had ascended to the ranks of the most generous, I gave a few rare gifts where I could. But I now realized I hadn't given enough. I had forgotten that I had taken a gift at all. It was freely given and freely taken in return, but it was wholly unreciprocated. Joan had given me the greatest gift of my life and I had done nothing in return for her or anyone else. I had ignored her completely and allowed myself to become surrounded by those who had never even seen me before I was someone to be seen. She was right to chastise me. This gift had cost me my generosity. I had become a taker and it was time to give again.

Even with the free time granted by the gifts of grades and papers, the desk had taken three straight weeks of labor. It was the most beautiful gift I had ever made: compact, lightweight, strong, with discrete cabinets and a beautiful blend of colors. Its manufacture had attracted more than a little attention and there was a small crowd gathered around me to see who was lucky enough to receive it.

I waved Joan over as she exited the tech. Her mess of tight curls shrouded her face, and I could hear the onlookers whisper "taker" as she came up to me.

"Joan, I would like to give you this desk. I can think of no one more worthy of it. You have given me many gifts over the years that I could never repay. Your gifts to this community, including your tireless work at

Three Oaks, are far too often overlooked. I hope this desk can help you in your studies and that it properly conveys my gratitude."

I had practiced the speech the night before. It was the same as what I had written in the official gift registry. The words were important. The gift wasn't just the desk itself, though it was no small thing, the real gift was my acknowledgment of her. My status gave those words serious weight. With one gift, I would hitch her to my rising star.

The tiny crowd froze behind me. They were as eager for Joan's response as I was. They were eager for her gratitude, eager to acknowledge her as someone worthy of such a spectacular gift.

But Joan didn't embrace me. She didn't cry tears of joy and clap her hands. She simply looked at the desk and said, "I don't need a desk," then walked past me and my tiny crowd. Over her shoulder, she shouted, "Give it to one of your pretty new friends."

The onlookers and I froze, and then snickering filled my ears as they petered out behind me. Cold tentacles of fear crawled up my back. No one refused a gift like this, whether they needed a desk or not. The real gift was far more than mahogany and brass hinges, it was my presence, acknowledgment, and friendship. She had turned all of these down without a second thought.

I had been wrong. Joan didn't want me to give again, to reciprocate to her and others as was right. That visit on the hill hadn't been a chastisement of my greed, but a reminder of what I owed. She alone had given me my new life and she alone knew it didn't belong to me. I owed Joan a massive debt, and she decided when it was paid.

Money is not something I'm used to dealing with. My food, my home, and the things that fill it are all gifts. Gifts given by people that knew I would give everything I could back in return. A family like mine had little use for ravs, we were generous enough to need only the generosity of others. So, it was beyond strange to be holding twenty ravs in my hand and even stranger to slip them through the slats of Joan's Tech locker. I'd sold the desk and half the gifts I'd received in the last few months to get the money, including an ornate candle holder Billy had carved himself and a crystal beaded necklace made by Eliza-Beth. I received strange looks when I sold these precious gifts for cash, but I'd had no choice. Joan had refused my gift and all that came with it. Joan was not simply content to let me live the life she had given me. She had shown me that much. She had no interest in sharing in the light of my generosity, but money was another story. Money could buy all the food, clothing, and comforts her family only received when someone pitied them or when the bone was full. They would still be takers, but fed takers, living takers.

The coins rattled as they fell into Joan's locker, and they rattled even louder when they spilled out of mine later that day. Heavy, loud, obnoxious things. Twenty ravs, enough money to buy her family food for a year and she gave them back like they were nothing. There was no note with my ravs returned to me. The only response was the money itself – a clear message that Joan would rather she and her family suffer than take anything from me. Even this small fortune couldn't buy me out of her debt.

Joan was attacking the floor with her mop when I arrived. She had already cleared the equipment, swept the entire facility, and begun mopping while sunlight still poured through the windows. I joined her from across the room, trying to match her pace. She didn't acknowledge me. After only five minutes with the thwack and splash of the mop to occupy my attention, my mind began to ache. I threw the mop down with a huff.

"What do you want?" I whimpered. "What do you want from me, Joan?"

She leaned her mop gently in the bucket and smiled. An ugly grin, all teeth. "Want from you? Surely the generous Ev would not be so base as to offer an exchange. If you offer a gift freely, I'm sure I will accept it freely."

"You didn't take the desk."

"I have no need for a desk."

"It was a gift.

"One I had no need for."

"You didn't take the ravs," I said.

She sneered. "The twenty ravs tossed in my locker without even a note? Surely that wasn't a gift. I'm not some taker rattling my cup at passers-by or crawling desperate to the bone. I don't want your money."

"Then what do you want, Joan? If you don't want gifts or credit or money, what do you want from me?"

"I want to finish cleaning, Ev. It takes twice as long without you here."

I looked down at my hands. Without my regular labor, they had lost all their long-held callouses and were aching already.

"Joan, you spread the rumors. You gave me the gift," I said.

Joan nodded. "And you took it. You took from Taye, desperate and greedy, just like all your pathetic lookers would have done. And now you call me taker behind my back."

I opened my mouth to protest, but I couldn't force the lie out. "I gave you a gift in return," I moaned.

"Keep your gifts, Ev. Keep your life. You earned it."

She turned and mopped her way out into the hallway. I tried to speak with her again, but she wouldn't even look at me. After a few minutes, I dumped out my mop bucket and left.

This time it was harder. My stock was still high, but my notoriety wasn't what it had once been. I'd sold all the gifts I'd acquired and begun laboring in a heavy-manufacturing plant. The looks to and from work stung, but I knew they were worth it. I needed the money and the labor it took to earn it. The gift from Joan hadn't been a gift at all and it hadn't been freely given. It was a yoke, one that tied me to Joan's crime for as long as I wore it. She was a credit thief. She had taken the credit that was rightfully Taye's and given it to me. And I accepted it without question and became the greatest taker the Tech has ever seen. And Joan knew it. She wouldn't take my gifts; she wouldn't accept my friendship. But she wasn't gone either. She stayed on the edge of my life, threatening it with every breath she took. If I couldn't convince her to join in the spoils of what we had taken from Taye, to mire herself as I had done, I would have to give what I had taken.

The news made the Tech even wilder this time. Sixty. Sixty ravs to the Bone and they were alive with the buzz of it. The work that must have taken. The respect hidden within. And before the end of the day, everyone knew who had done it: two quiet takers named Taye and Joan.

I was relieved. Tired and relieved. My own stock had fallen far after news of me working for wages had got out. I now stood little better than I had before all this began, but I had repaid the gift in kind. I had done the work and given back what I owed. And now Taye would receive the credit he truly deserved, and Joan would receive credit for a gift she hadn't given. She would become a taker, same as I had been, and I would be free. This was a gift she could never refuse, not without harming Taye who had done nothing but give.

I had been freed from her debt and the relief settled over me and flushed the shame from my core. I had given so much of myself, not only my labor, but the credit, gifts, and status I had always wanted. And now I was a taker no longer. I was excited to see no one waiting for me as I exited my classes. I was relieved at the prospect of cleaning Three Oaks tonight. Everything was as it should be.

I found Billy and Eliza-Beth standing in front of my locker at fifth bell. They, like all the other lookers, hadn't spoken to me for months. Today they came up to me fawning, delicate, and smelling of roses.

"We heard what you did," one of them said. Then all of them said it, one by one. All the lookers. Then all the instructors. Then everyone else. Joan had set the record straight. She had told them about all the money I'd given and how I had tried to give her and Taye credit. They surrounded me at the steps of the Tech. Thousands of them. I could even see my parents in the crowd. A hundred ravs to the Bone in under a year. An enormous sum given to those few dared give to and I hadn't even kept the credit. I had thrown it away like it was nothing to two people who could hardly have deserved it. I was more than a giver. I was a legend reborn. I was fantastic. I was nothing they'd ever seen before.

Joan stood at the edge of the crowd. She wore a smile, a sad one that only pulled at the edges of her mouth. Twice now she had openly refused my generous gift freely given.

She was an ingrate of the highest order and an ungrateful taker at that. She had taken on a status so low she could never crawl out from under it. She would likely never receive another gift again, but she held no debt. She had ruined herself rather than become a taker like me. I stared at her while the crowd pawed at me. She had given me another gift. One far too large. One I couldn't refuse or ever repay. I was fantastic now and forever. I was a taker, now and forever.

I saw Taye join Joan at the edge of the crowd. They smiled at each other, the kind of smiles that could light up a room.

Connor Mellegers is a freelance writer living in Toronto. When not writing speculative fiction, you can find them reading, cooking, and struggling to grow a garden.

The Wyldblood 10th issue 10 Best lists

10 best fantasy TV

The Walking Dead
Shadow and Bone
Game of Thrones
The Witcher
House of the Dragon
The Sandman
Outlander
Carnival Row
His Dark Materials
Sweet Tooth

10 best superhero TV

The Umbrella Academy
Jessica Jones
Daredevil
The Boys
Loki
WandaVision
The Falcon and the Winter Soldier
Watchmen
Batman (1960s)
Agents of SHIELD

Crimson Redux

Janna Miller

Jennie arranged what had once been petticoats into layers of tattered brown and waited in twilight for the methane gas lamps to come alive. Anyone with the slightest Ability would agree a crowded city was the worst place to do any tracking - even if most of those born differently were created in the shantytowns which rose from the steaming rivers snaking nearby. And New Atlanta was worse than most, with acrid smells of horse dung and despair emanating from almost every corner.

Flashes of insight jumbled in Jennie's mind, mixing all the hopes and fears of the sweaty masses. Still, she pushed through the dense psychic residue to follow every lead, explore every misplaced hunch. She gathered and documented the slightest itch and tingle. Triangulating senses where she could, she worked her way all through New Atlanta's cobblestone streets in mismatched, ill-fitting shoes, searching for the faintest trace of her girl. The one she'd let slip away.

Eventually, her overstrained Ability led her to one neighborhood in particular, following tendrils of muddy pastels only Jennie could perceive. Houses here were dressed in high columns and spiked iron fences, with expansive, droid-cut lawns. There was nothing subtle in the suburb of Peachblossom - and it was nearly impossible to infiltrate, unless you were willing to get filthy in every sense. Which Jennie already was.

Pops sounded in succession as flames erupted in their iron cages, illuminating the length of the avenue. Jennie wiped her face with an inner sleeve and pulled at the strings of her bonnet before shambling up to the gate of the nearest house, her wares trailing in a wagon behind her. She and her kind were only accepted without appointment at night, when polite society retired to the upper rooms. Faint chimes echoed inside when she pulled a bell-cord to a white columned estate, greenery pruned into squares and straight lines.

For a moment, she thought curls of red smoke oozed from an upstairs window, but it was probably nothing. So many false leads over the last months weighed her down in blood and bone.

Others with the Ability would not help her. Solitary, divided to grapple for scant resources, the best of them were picked off by the wealthy, to conjure and entertain. The worst, well, the worst did whatever they could to survive.

The butler opened a massive oak door and paraded down the brick walk in long, metallic strides. Programmed to mimic distaste, he raised his eyebrows and stared down his perfect grey nose.

"State your business."

"Muckraker, number 263. I heard the Master might be looking for artifacts." She waved at the cart behind her.

"License."

Jennie lifted a sleeve to show her city issued tattoo, done in cheap blue indigo that blurred at the edges and feathered into her skin. The butler scanned it and led her around the main house to a shed in the back.

"Lay your wares on the table." He armed the poisoned darts kept pinned on his lapel as a matter of routine security, and trained them on Jennie's heart.

Reaching into her cart, she pulled out a handful of ancient coins, a dirt encrusted necklace, and a statue of an ugly little man with a painted red hat that was, for some reason, all the rage.

The butler clicked in a way she knew meant he was interested.

"Found it in the rushes by the south bend. Almost perfect. Only ten doubloons. It's a steal really."

The butler knew it was, and without asking the house for authorization, reached for the money purse he kept inside his right kneecap. Jennie held out a bag of her own, indicating he drop the payment in.

Just as his metal fingers made contact with the sack, the lights behind his eyes dimmed to nothing and his gears froze. The magnetized fabric hung over his partially extended fingers while Jennie took two steps back, prodding his immobile arm.

She had killed him, if only for a little while.

Five minutes and a screwdriver later, the butler's detached left hand let Jennie in the back door. Breathing the climatized-cool air brought gooseflesh to her arms and reminded her of younger, darker days. Days she would not wish on anyone. Better to sell trinkets and be free.

Except now the only bit of real beauty and actual value she had been allowed in this life had been stolen. Or manipulated. Either way, the result was the same. And the stakes were so high.

Absorbing the stillness by the back door, clear images rose in Jennie's mind for the first time in months. Something small, but important waited in the next room.

She sensed a living presence near it. Not unfriendly, she realized, just another tired yellow aura. Probably a maid tidying up before bed. From the doorway, Jennie pushed through the yellow of the woman's mind, sorting through images until she found a mass of exhaustion. Jennie put gentle pressure on the psychic collection near her sleep nerve until the servant's body fell to the carpet with a muffled thud.

Entering the room and stepping carefully over the now sleeping body, Jennie caught her breath. Slim, purple tendrils beckoned to her from a chair in the corner, like streaming dark ink spooling through water. They floated in the air, the longest strings brushing her face in a way that made Jenny lose her heart with longing. These remnants of her daughter.

It was difficult to be confronted with this trace of her after so long. Jennie fell to her knees and reached forward blindly, pulling something soft from the crevice of an upholstered brocade chair. She stuffed it in her pocket and backed out of the house as quickly as her legs allowed, retrieving her muddy shoes by the back door.

Forcing her breathing into a slow rhythm, she re-attached the butler's hand with shaking fingers and deactivated the magnet at the bottom of the sack. He reanimated with a rush of gears and released the money he had been clutching for much longer than he realized.

"That's all for tonight then. You are welcome back if you find anything else of value. Otherwise, don't waste my time." He turned on his heel, as he had been programmed to do.

Jennie's legs shook as she pulled her wagon from the back of the massive estate and down the walk, tripping over the curb into the gas-lit street. She kept her pace until she paused under a bridge she knew to be safe from view. Her pocket erupted in lavender when she pulled out the bundle she had retrieved from the chair, enveloping her with a soft, gentle peace. It unfolded into a handkerchief, edged with embroidered spring flowers. Jennie pressed it to her nose.

Breathing her daughter in. Knowing for certain she was still alive. Or was, earlier today. *Cecily.*

Jennie spent the afternoon knee deep in mud on the banks of a swampy creek, feeling through the layers of muck for treasures beneath her feet. The biggest prizes lay deposited deep in the silt of ages and uncovered only with the work of sticks or shovels. Though mechanics were her forte, she could sense the emotional pull of other lost things appealing to the Masters and Mistresses. Antiques and trinkets, tossed into the river or mislaid there years before. Pushed by tidal currents to finally lodge themselves in alluvial plains and tributaries.

A muddy pile of lumpy objects grew beside her as the sun dripped down the sky. Dodging mosquitoes, she rinsed her clothes and finds upstream, dispelling the smell of brine. Her dress had mostly dried by the time night fell, dampness lingering at her waist and under her arms.

As she approached the largest house near the middle of the street, the moon emerged between clouds, illuminating acres of white stucco walls. This time, when she pulled the cord, a single, deep gong rang from inside the massive edifice. Manicured shrubbery near the door shivered with the vibrations.

The butler that answered could have been the twin of the one from the night before in dress and manner, except for the especially heavy starch of his collar. It was easy enough to deactivate him after Jennie presented the mostly intact antique Blueware vase she offered for pittance. Wouldn't the Mistress be pleased?

When she opened the servant's door, the smell that reached under the cool, processed air was that of death. Enough blood to block her from perceiving much of anything else. Nearly frozen by the hanging coats and umbrellas, she stepped into a sensory storm that dulled even the touch of her skin. Entering the house would mean she would do so blindly, most of her Ability dulled. But not finding out what lay inside could be worse.

Under swirls of hovering and departing auras, she could at least sense no one remained alive downstairs. She moved to the kitchens, one toe after another, just two doors down.

Three servants lay in pools on the tile floor, each one face-down and twisted. She dipped a finger into the spreading red. Still warm.

Reflexively, she shook her hand, flinging the cloying droplet into the red mass moving towards her shoes. The tide of blood and psychic echoes of recent death closed in on Jennie's mind, nearly crippling her. Horror etched each breath with a panic that stripped her throat raw.

Wheezing, she backed away from the dead, struggling to replace the image before her with the embroidered handkerchief stuffed in her pocket. With Cecily's soft brown eyes. She must keep going.

Palming a knife from the countertop, Jennie moved past the working areas to the front sitting room, barely allowing the disturbance of her shaking hands. Velvet chairs and arranged flowers reflected as soft as a painting in the dim light. A ticking clock muffled against plush carpet and thick drapery. In the air, traces of purple floated in the dust motes, casting a twilight glow. Cecily had been here recently and frequently, but left nothing else behind.

Under the horror, a minute sense of relief flooded into her crevasses and stiff muscles: Cicely was not part of this carnage. Wherever else she might be, she was not downstairs now.

Even more alarming even than the bodies in the kitchen, were the strands of crimson aura that wove through the room, especially thick at the settee and on one antique rose-china teacup. As they floated, extended tendrils wrapped around the lamp, the leg of a chair, a doorknob, letting go to encircle something else. One brushed lightly against her throat and imperceptibly tightened before she stepped back, out of reach.

They reminded her of the traces she got off caged animals in the zoo. The ones that were quiet and docile until someone's hand came too close to the bars. And they reminded her, most disturbingly, of someone she once knew.

Someone who should have been long dead.

Stopping by the stairs to the bedrooms, the crimson aura darkened, almost dripping down the stairwell. Fresh. Too much for her to ascertain anything except bloody rust from the upper floors. Jennie fled then, abandoning the carnage cooling in the kitchen.

She revived the butler, accepted payment and shambled away.

Extra cautious, she slept behind the opera house, where there would always be someone to hear her scream.

The police questioned her the next morning, having reviewed the butler's corrupted files. They were pointed in asking if she had seen or heard anything, but did not ask if she had been inside the house. Her throat still raw, she wrung her hands until the officer rolled his eyes and dismissed her. From where she stood across the road, Jennie could just spy stretchers carrying out four forms under four stained sheets. One more person than she had stumbled upon the night before. When the last body emerged, Jennie was nearly crippled with psychic wailing that escaped the house's airtight windows. Peeling back the raw emotion in her mind, she sensed a wave of cold fear mixed with the deepest grief.

She skipped the muckraking that afternoon and perched on a hidden bench at the edge of the neighborhood, probing into the estates as best she could. Further than she had ever been able to. Cecily must be nearby, possibly in one of the houses on this street - her frightened presence now keenly apparent. The flashes Jennie could discern from around her daughter were consistent: a white dress, a disheveled bed. And blood.

That night, Jennie pulled her cart along the cobblestones to the last house on the street. Crimson blotted the front doorway and the butler walked through it unknowingly, sending off ominous eddies. When he scanned her tattoo, he did not invite her back to show her wares. Instead, he pulled out an envelope, sealed with red wax. After handing it to her, the butler disappeared back into the house, shutting the double-hung door with a final click of the lock.

Jennie broke the seal in the street, right where she stood, to read the message inside. Smooth cream paper reflected the fluttering lamplight.

The honor of your presence is requested
On Saturday, the 7th of June at 5 o'clock.
A SEANCE
hosted by Madame Locke
Tea precedes the ceremony

Formal attire required.

A presence in the house seemed to press on Jennie's shoulders as she read. Turning back to the imposing white edifice, red emanated from the top right window, like a slow bleed.

Stirring from her makeshift bed the next morning, Jennie spied Cecily from the bottom of the bridge, surprising her out of a morning stupor. Jennie stuffed bonnet ties into her mouth to keep from calling out. Her eyes fixated on the precious form now moving with haste across a narrow stone span above.

Cecily's strawberry hair flew out behind her, barely contained behind a stiff white hat trimmed in taffeta and silk flowers. She had grown some, and Jennie had the uncomfortable sensation of not knowing her own daughter's exact details. Two older women flanked her, attempting to keep up with the girl's brisk stride. Their dull brown auras meant nothing good. As handlers, they could do little besides follow crude orders, though they could protect their charge against Jennie well enough.

It would not work, she knew, to try to get Cecily now. And for all she could tell, if she made contact, her daughter would be bustled off somewhere else. Jennie would have to start all over again, painstakingly moving through the city street by street. And time was working against her.

Cecily's purple aura shone as bright as when she was a child, even when she had been covered in mud digging along the riverbank.

Sweet Princess Cecily, Heir to the Muck. She would laugh when Jennie addressed her like that.

"If I am a Princess, you are the Queen."

Jennie had pulled from the mud a brass belt buckle that could shine if she polished it. "I am absolutely the Queen. A figurehead with no subjects and no power. Just lots and lots of mud."

She paused to capture a mental picture of the girl, growing so fast, and wished for something better. A safe place for her to live in, a school, friends. Where she didn't have to spend her days in the river, ankles perpetually wet with the filthy silt of centuries.

Jennie smiled for her daughter, pushing away impossibilities. The world did not work for people like them, it never had. "We are fine though, the two of us. We have a room, food, and all the mud of the world. What else could we need?"

Cecily dreamed into the distance for a moment, a streak of drying silt on her right cheek. "If I went to the parlors, I bet I could change things. I bet I could help us. Maybe even all of us." She knew as muckrakers, they were not alone. She gestured to the other shabby figures, bent over bits of mud around them. Feeling below for whatever would lead them to their next meal.

Jennie's retort had, in retrospect, been overly harsh. "Never!" Cecily startled with the intensity. Jennie threw a digging stick she had been holding, lobbing it with a splash in the middle of the water. Cecily froze, her eyes wide as river stones. "Never even think about it! There is no place in there for you! In the houses they are cruel and thoughtless. I promise you, they are too much for you to handle. They are too much for all of us!"

Jennie should never have told Cecily about the cakes before meals began, or the pressed cotton sheets. Or the dresses and scented baths. Especially that Cecily wasn't up to working in the parlors. Instead, she should have mentioned that most who entertained did so at the peril of their souls. That most girls with Ability who wore the white dresses did not get to enjoy them for long.

Under her flowered hat, Cecily wore a white dress now.

Jennie lost sight of her daughter as she moved off the bridge and down the street. She cried under the stone arch for a long while. Wondering, had she done something more in that moment, if Cecily would still be with her. Still digging in the mud and huddling next to her at night against the cold.

When she could no longer trace any of her daughter's sweet aura swirling along the bridge, Jennie dried her face. After all, a mother's job was to protect, even if the child didn't know it. Even if that child might be bonded to someone else now. She had a duty to try to keep her from harm. And offer to take the pain, in her stead.

She stored her cart behind azalea bushes, taking the best jewelry and all the wealth she had ever acquired. The early morning was spent running errands - buying things instead of scrounging for them, from second hand stores. As the day wore on, she added to her appearance, layering only the hint of an illegal glamour to her face and pocketbook.

In a stuffy upstairs room, Jennie signed a contract with a silver fountain pen, looking not at all like the pauper queen of a riverbank. Fake references, fake clothes and pedigree, but the lawyer took enough money to overlook any discrepancies. That, and a promise of a half-buried bottle of brandy, aged in the heart of the Chattahoochee River itself.

What she bought at the last stop of the afternoon, she put inside a small metal holder, carefully snapping it shut. Just in case she was still alive at the end of the day.

At four forty-five, Jennie walked the cobblestones of Peachblossom in the daylight. She remembered not to slouch, not to shamble, but to hold her head up high. She would not be arriving in a coach like the others, but she would still arrive in style. Artifice was mostly about attitude, another lesson from long ago.

She did not need to ring the bell, the door opened before her. She held the invitation in her gloved hand, placing it on the silver tray the butler proffered. As she stepped into the house, Jennie's knees buckled and she steadied herself on a table in the foyer. The

scarlet aura choked in a thick fog. So thick, it took a minute to find her balance and wrap a last bit of protection around herself. She smiled outwardly and prepared for the onslaught when she saw the woman glance around the room.

Madame Locke did not recognize Jennie, now that she was grown. The white-haired woman must have thought only that Jennie competed for territory when she proffered the invitation. Had wanted to toy with her and drain her for fuel, like the others.

Covered in garnets and dripping lace shawls, Madame Locke greeted most guests with a nod. The woman appeared just as Jennie remembered, a docile creature with fangs and claws hidden just behind her clothes. Smiling, bowing her head while welling, oozing scarlet. Just as she had for more than a century. Jennie wondered why the others in the room could not feel the menace.

A maid in a white lace apron rang a bell for tea and ladies moved as one into the dining room. The long table was filled with tiers of pastries and fruit, mechanized to rotate past each seat. Jennie made for the far end, hoping the towering food would help keep her glamour hidden for a little longer. Each moment Madame Locke could not account for Jennie's true nature was time she could put to good use.

Madame sat at the opposite end of the table, watching the other women pick at prepared delicacies. Closest to her was the owner of the house, followed by a series of frilly dresses, and a woman wearing a black veil. On Madame's right side, of course, was Cecily, still donned in white, her eyes cast downward and solemn. Did she know yet, that she was the lamb?

Jennie struggled against running to her daughter and embracing her, from dragging her out the room and away from the imminent, swirling-red tendrils of danger. She longed to touch her face for the first time in a year, to bury her head in her sweet hair, and to share the desperation of her absence - every hour, every minute.

Soon, dear Cecily. If all goes well.

Small talk lasted for half an hour and Jennie held her own. No one questioned her presence in a blue satin dress, or would ever guess she had sold them trinkets and walked their lower floors in the night. Or even, that she understood more about these parlor games than they could ever guess.

Finally, the mountain of moving food was cleared away, and Madame Locke rose, nodding at the servants to close the curtains and light the black candles. As her eyes caught Jennie's, she smiled with predator's teeth. Her voice started like low thunder in the distance, rumbling over them all.

"Ladies. Thank you for coming today. I know many of you are here out of curiosity, though several of you are looking for something. Something gone. Something beyond us. Even a recent loss. I hope that, with our collective energies, we can find things today as well. And just maybe," here her voice took on notes of the coming storm, "We will have answers that we desire."

Madame Locke leaned forward. "I have been among you for a short time, evaluating your needs, interviewing you, living in your rooms. My reputation as the city's strongest psychic is not unwarranted. I ask that you remove your gloves and grasp hands. Let the mood take you where it will. I will lead."

Right to the pits of hell, thought Jennie.

As soon as clammy hands connected and the human circuit completed, a buzz of electricity hummed through their fingers. Jennie channeled some to a battery she wore in a belt under her dress, an old trick of hers. Madame Locke had been unchallenged for so long, she had forgotten anyone could, however crudely. Or maybe she did remember, having lured Cecily from the river too.

Madame's voice rose as she chanted the elemental opening phrases of the seance. Calling on those present to lend energy before she pierced the veil aside. Immediately, Jennie felt the electricity pull from her as it coursed through her body. Murmurs around the table indicated the others were uncomfortable in giving so much, but were too polite to object. The first battery full, Jennie fed energy to another.

Madame called into the void and it responded. She was as good as she claimed, better even than Jennie remembered. She asked questions from those present and received answers from the dead. Twice possessed by other spirits, she allowed her body to be used to communicate. Unknown to the others in the room, the recently dead souls hovered behind her in a vigilant circle, ironically clinging to the one who brought them down.

Jennie recognized the once-still bodies from the kitchen, centered in their own warm blood. Two women and one man, wearing blank expressions and the servant's clothes they died in. Each one had a hand nailed to the Madame's crimson aura, dripping what little essence they had left into the cloud, feeding it. Behind them, winds of the dark void lashed against their backs, buffeting them against their tether.

Nestled in front, almost protectively, was another figure. Young and wearing what once must have been a fine lace nightgown before it had been torn to shreds. She appeared strikingly like Cecily, had this figure not been dead. Long hair cascaded down her back, framing dark, pooling eyes. Both of her hands rested on Madame's shoulders. The color of her pale pink aura fading with each moment.

Madame's cheeks flushed with seeming vigor as she was filled, pausing before the next question from the room could be asked. She turned her eyes to each of those near her end of the circle.

And then she took her due.

The red aura moved around the room, touched each hand and rested on each head. Taking a bit of life to pay for the time

Madame borrowed from death - extending her time on Earth like a parasite that would not die. She filled her desiccated aura with the essence of those around her.

Except for Jennie. Madame glanced across the table and noted something different about her, as more than a woman with some Ability. And understood. She was missing the mud, the rags, and the smell. Jennie had disguised herself among the flounces and whale boned corsets, but now shone with an aura of diamonds. As clear as when she was a child - but now unfettered, uncompromised, and filled with righteous anger.

The one that got away, slinking back into the swamps to hide. Madame's only loose end.

Cecily noticed her at the same time, finally seeing past her clothes and artifice as a brilliant beacon. She rose in her chair, and weakly turned toward the end of the table. "Mama?"

Madame paused for only a measured heartbeat before she tightened white knuckles, her lips pulled into a tight, vengeful half-smile. Recognizing an opportunity.

Cecily fell into her chair, writhing in pain. Jennie felt Madame target her, pushing her closer to the veil and the dead souls that hovered there, eager to use her young life as a stepping stone to return to the world. The betrayal in Cecily's eyes hurt like Jennie's had, at her age. When she realized she was just a pawn. That there was no escape from her Ability. She would never be free here, no matter what she had been promised.

If Jennie broke the circle now, she might not be able to save her daughter. Only Madame could stop it without harm, so close to the void. But Jennie could alter the conduit. Instead of adding her essence, Jennie added her voice, pitched so the ladies of the room could perceive it as vibrations under manicured fingernails.

shelivesoffthebloodofothers she lives off the blood of others shelivesofftheboodofothers

The women cocked their heads and glanced up and down the table, unsuccessfully searching for the source of the vibrations that did not seem to match the seance around them. Eyelids fluttered.

Jennie did not know who Madame had killed up the stairs that night, but the ghost of the girl that appeared so like Cecily, faced the older woman draped in black veils with palpable longing.

Madame had meant it to be Cecily, of course. To take her protege's blood price in an ancient, but messy way. Jennie's vision of the tangled bedsheets at the park bench had shown Jennie that belatedly. If only Jennie could have sensed over the blood when she entered the house two nights before, she could have rescued her then.

Madame's aura filled the room so that everyone seemed covered in a red haze. The other ladies chittered in alarm, finally understanding something was off. Jennie measured their wild heartbeats through the energy that kept their hands tightly locked together. Cecily drooped like a white flower, losing her will. But Madame was nervous.

thegirlstandsbehindherkiller the girl stands behind her killer thegirlstandsbehindherkiller

This time, Jennie's message rang clear to everyone in the group. Heads turned and many murmured under their breaths. The woman in the black veil fidgeted and fought against the current. She regarded Madame with a dawning cold.

"Did you...kill my servants? Did you kill my daughter?" The red mist cleared from above her head. "Did you kill Olivia?" The woman in black's voice took on some of the thunder that had been Madame's. In that second, the ancient psychic faltered.

And it was enough. In the space of an indrawn breath, Jennie emptied the contents of all three of the batteries she had collected, pushing at Madame's sleep nerve and essence all at once. The red riled around her, fighting the energy. A wind and a howl moved around the room.

The three spirits closest to the void pulled their hands free as her aura pulsated. In an instant, they sailed into the void and were consumed.

The last form clung to Madame against the wind, the bloodied girl. She moved her hands from her killer's shoulders to around her throat. Forcing her essence between the older woman's teeth. She turned Madame's head to the woman in black and spoke formally, like an upper-class debutante.

"So sorry, Mother. I would have liked to spend more time here. I'll wait for you, just on the other side. Give my love to Father."

She let go, spinning backward until she disappeared. The void expanded as she entered, like a giant splash of a boulder into water. It seemed to replace the drawing room with a swirling pool that now sucked at the tendril ends of Madame's red aura, infusing them with the deepest dark.

Struggling to breathe, Madame opened her mouth. With each gasp, the red rushed in and consumed her. Drowning her from within. Veins exploded under her skin, pooling in her eyes and at her joints. Turning as dark as the hole behind her. Her skin mummified and blackened, shriveling with the age she had stolen.

As the circle broke, a sudden fetid wind moved through the room, extinguishing the candles.

What remained of Madame was still; the last blood price her own.

Shaking blackened dust off her hand, Cecily reached towards Jennie for the first time in a year. Her voice weak, but alive. "You came for me."

Everyone else still frozen in the darkness, Jennie threw back her chair and finally embraced her daughter before another breath could be taken, folding sweet lavender scent into her arms. She did not know how she would let go of her again.

And yet she needed to, just briefly. To keep her daughter safe for the long term, there was one more thing Jennie needed to do. Cecily had been right, that day along the river bank – if they were smart, they could change things. They could live without fear.

Jennie rose from her knees and opened the metal case she had picked up earlier, as the women shook and stirred. Cicely clung to her mother's waist as Jennie placed a card in front of each of the figures along the table, hands no longer joined. She lit new, white candles from the sideboard, illuminating the destroyed room: paintings and vases lay in shards along the oriental rugs, the tablecloth torn much like the murdered girl's nightdress.

The women avoided Madame's corpse to follow Jennie's progress around the room, though they would not meet her eyes. All except the woman in black, her grief emanating with a cold anger. After circling the table, Jennie stood before the door, clutching again at Cicely.

"Ladies, my strength lies in psychic mechanics, while Madame's was in blood. This," she gestured to the blackened remains of their former parlor royalty, "has happened over and over to the poor with Ability. Usually, it is us who die for your ends. For your entertainment. I am sorry for your losses. So sorry." Jennie whispered the last to the stiff-backed woman in black. "However, if you have need of our services, my information is on my card. I suggest you take it."

The flowers on Jennie's hat shook slightly for the first time that afternoon. This was not sneaking into houses, or reprogramming droids to erase small crimes. Nor was this charging more than she should on certain found items so she could eat. It was not even confronting the most dangerous woman in New Atlanta in a bid to save her child.

She was about to go toe to toe with a social order that had not changed for centuries. She had a solution against the parlors, though it was, in many ways, unpleasant medicine. She hoped it would be enough. For her, for Cecily, for the others abused and discarded for trinkets and entertainment.

She tugged at one glove and let her eyes wander the room to the undamaged velvet cushions the women sat on and the fine diamond necklaces they wore. To the shining upended goblets and decanters, they drank from.

To Cecily's bloodshot eyes, contrasting with her once-pristine white dress, now smudged with black.

Exhaustion running through Jennie's bones, she straightened her back and lifted her chin over the group. There was one more thing she needed to say. "I am opening a psychic consultation service in Five Points in the next few days. Bonded contracts and payments for every job. I expect many of our kind will follow me. We are done with servitude and the abuse that comes from our place in your lives. Either along the river, or in your homes. Neither will you be taken in by the likes of Madame Locke again. If you want something, you will know where to find us."

Not waiting for a reply, Jennie strode from the room, taking her daughter with her from the house. The ladies fingered her card with some trepidation, unsure whether they had been used or saved. In the end, Jennie counted on them preferring the businesswoman over the demon. Payments of money instead of blood.

To keep her daughter safe today, and in the future.

Cecily leaned into her mother as they walked, intertwining lavender and crystal. "I am so sorry, I…"

Jennie stopped her. "It happened to me too. Who am I to fault you for doing the same?"

Cecily's lips trembled and she gripped her mother's hand more tightly. "I thought I could change things. I was sure it would work."

She smoothed her daughter's hair and kissed her brow. "Maybe now it can."

"Will you really be a Queen, Mama, with your own domain?"

"If others follow us, then maybe something like it. You were right, of course. It's past time to make things better for ourselves. Surely the other muckrakers will see that banding together will keep us safe. After all...we know where all the old bones are, and who put them there."

Jennie glanced back at the windows of the darkened parlor of the house behind them. "It's time people remembered that."

Jennie hugged her daughter just outside on the cobblestone street and did not stop. Not for a long time. Hand in hand, they retrieved their old cart from beneath the trees and traveled to the center of the city, turning left when a tangle of five streets met. Carrying their old wares, they climbed iron stairs to a purple painted door. Jennie fished a key from her purse and entered a set of dusty rooms, activating an older model security robot behind them.

On the balcony they could sense the city's fear and despair, though it wasn't quite as intense so high up. From here, they could follow the trail they made walking together from Peachblossom, stretching out along the road into the distance.

Bright and clear and free of mud.

⸻⸻◇⸻⸻

Janna Miller has been published with Andromeda Spaceways, Daily Science Fiction, and Smokelong Quarterly, among others.

The Blessing of Lady Charlotte

Mark Rigney

Mother's decline was much more rapid than she'd hoped, and we never had time to finish our lessons. I don't blame her. Even our kind is not entirely immune to disease, and from the moment she realized she was sick, she tried to teach me everything she knew.

I look back now, and I realize that my frantic attempts to step, fully fledged, into Mother's many roles was a desperate gambit to ignore her absence. It's what people today call a "coping mechanism." And I had no father, or at least not one to know—none of our kind do—and no siblings, either. It was just me, all of twelve years old, and my lonely house full of very demanding mirrors.

Nights were the worst. Being woken by an active mirror is like being splashed with a bucket of ice water, from the inside out. The sensation doesn't last (unless you don't respond) but in the moment? It's awful. How Mother managed it all those years, or Gran before her? I cannot imagine.

Actually, I know perfectly well how they handled the sacred duty of tending our mirrors. They'd completed the training. They'd learned to sleep through all but the actual emergencies, which were in fact few and far between. I, however, was four years too young to be doing what I was doing, and while I'd been sensitized—oh ye Gods, was I sensitized—I lacked control. Finesse. The ability to block the mirrors' cries.

Lady Charlotte, far away in Lathom House, nearly did me in all on her own. She was French-born, but had been married off to a certain James Stanley, the seventh Earl of Derby. No doubt he was a decent enough man, but now he was away, ordered north to fight the Scots, and Lady Charlotte found herself besieged by a stick-in-the-mud Roundhead by the name of Sir Thomas Fairfax. Lathom House—a castle, really, with perimeter fortifications, nine towers, six-foot walls, and a proper moat—was suddenly surrounded by two thousand hostile troops.

Did Lady Charlotte surrender? No. With a garrison of three hundred, she considered her options, found them lacking or at least unattractive, and went straight to her mirror.

What her family ever did to warrant owning one of our mirrors, I'll never know, but I doubt it had anything to do with Lady Charlotte herself. She struck me from the first as overbearing and arrogant. Still, I was obliged to help. All but catatonic from lack of sleep, I stumbled to Lady Charlotte's companion mirror, a pearl-inlaid hand-glass, more than a mite gaudy for my taste, and spoke.

"How," I said, trying to sound grown-up, "may I assist?"

"*Dieu soit félicité*," she responded, her voice so throaty that it made me imagine Lady Charlotte herself as quite heavy— which, as I later learned, she was. In lightly inflected English, she said, "My home is surrounded. I require a strategy for defeating my husband's enemies."

"I am the mirror," I said, "and I will aid she who owns the mirror. Tell me all."

I spoke imperiously, just as Mother had taught me, since a certain pomp is required for magic of our sort to work. Suspension of disbelief, they call it now.

Lady Charlotte laid out the details, much of which was beyond me. What did I know, from my elusive, hidden isle, of Cromwell, the Long Parliament, and the vagaries of England's bloody civil war?

"Hold," I said, in as lordly a tone as I could muster. I could only hope that the mirror, as Mother claimed it always did, was amplifying and deepening my voice. Otherwise, Lady Charlotte might quickly become suspicious, although I doubted she would ever discover that she was talking to a snip of a twelve-year-old hiding away in a tottering cliff-top villa overlooking the Tyrrhenian Sea.

I let go of my link with Lady Charlotte's mirror, ignored an incoming plea from a Russian girl mooning over some ne'er-do-well shepherd, and opened myself to the mirrors' collective power.

It is the oddest feeling, attuning oneself to time. Poetic descriptions of time—that it's a river and so on—are downright inaccurate when it comes to experiencing time's flow beyond one's normal place within it. I might say that it's like tumbling through breakers on a beach, or that it's reminiscent of drifting off to sleep (you become lulled, misted over, pulled under), but in the end I can say only that the experience is both singular and disturbing, unpleasant in the same manner as realizing you have failed to understand something vital, and that your failure will be ongoing. So it is with anyone who conjoins with time, for doing so goes against the natural order, as most magic does. Opening oneself to time breaks the ironbound laws of the cosmos, as the stomach-lurching queasiness that comes after will always attest.

Nevertheless, and despite all my disclaimers, casting oneself into time does provide exceptionally pertinent information.

So. I opened myself, concentrating on Lady Charlotte and her distant castle home. A minute or so later, I pulled myself back, threw up violently in the nearest of several buckets kept for exactly that purpose, and composed myself to once again speak with Lady Charlotte.

"Here," I said, "is what you must do. You will delay, and delay again. You will accept Fairfax's ambassadors, but you will treat them with disdain, for this will encourage your own forces. You will demand of Fairfax's lackeys a week in which to answer. When the week is up, demand a second. When Fairfax refuses, pick the best men of your garrison and send them out to sabotage your attackers' batteries. Do so repeatedly, under cover of night, or fog, or other distractions such as you may devise. If you do these things, the Eagle Tower of Lathom House shall not fall. Help will arrive at the end of June, with a superior force commanded by Prince Rupert of the Rhine. So take heart, Lady. Good fortune will yet be yours."

Generally, my supplicants are thankful when their mirror offers the future on a platter. Not Lady Charlotte. "*Je ne peux pas attendre jusqu'à juin!*" she exclaimed. "That is too long!"

I took a moment to heave out what little was left in my stomach, then said, "Lady, I am the Oracle of the Mirror, and I have spoken."

She cursed at me in French, German, and English, then flounced away. Or so I imagined. Certainly, she ceased staring at her hand-mirror. I let out a whale of a yawn and crept back to bed.

Most people do not abuse their mirrors, perhaps because, no matter their personal greed, they've been raised on cautionary tales of genies in bottles or disastrous wishes with invisible strings attached. Thus the owners of our companion mirrors rarely rely on them with any constancy. Nor do they typically ask the larger existential questions of "How will I die?" "When will I die?" or, worse, "When will my loved ones die?"

As Mother put it, "I can answer, if I must. But I do not wish to. My answers rarely bring happiness." Perhaps that is why she did not cast ahead and foresee her own demise (centuries early). If only she had!

Lady Charlotte, however, had been cut from more ungrateful cloth. Every day, for the next three weeks, she addressed her hand-glass, wanting answers for the most ridiculous, petty fancies. In what dress should she appear for dinner? Would it be prudent to replace her butler, whom she suspected of pilfering Lord Stanley's snuff? What should she do when she ran out of caviar, as she surely would by Friday?

As a rule, we only give our mirrors to those who have helped us down the years, but sometimes the apple falls far from the tree, and the child is not always worthy of the parent. Sometimes, too, mirrors fall into the

wrong hands, and if the new owner somehow learns the correct mode of address, well. There we are, my family line and I, the world's only true Oracles. Loyal custodians that we are, we answer those who call.

Not that Lady Charlotte was the only one abusing my time, but the others were more humble. Take Kula, for example, who had a gorgeous shell-framed mirror, square, and lived on the shores of the Niger River in what European cartographers of the day called Lower Ethiopia. She'd inherited her looking-glass, indirectly, from Askia the Great of Songhai, and she had a lot of questions about what it meant to be Islamic, poor, and hunted by white slavers who each year pressed farther upriver. I suggested her family get away from the river and any other obvious conduits for the slave trade. She said her father would not move. I told her she had seven months to convince him. After that, it would be too late.

"I am only thirteen," she said to me. "How am I supposed to impose my will on my father?"

And I replied, as only a twelve-year-old can, one who is very far away and utterly safe, "You will forecast a swarm of bees in ten days' time. The bees are a sign that you, too, must uproot yourselves and move on. The mirror has spoken."

One day before the bees were to swarm— which they would, I had splattered another bucket in foreseeing it—Kula called again. She said, "What if my father finds out about you, my mirror? And what if he says you are not of Allah?"

Luckily, Gran and Mother had long ago coached me on how to answer this one. "I am neither of Allah, nor not of Allah," I told Kula. "I am the Oracle."

I could almost hear her nodding sadly, alone in her home. Poor thing. Down the years, I have said much the same about Brigid, Jesus, Jehovah, and Moroni. For my part, Rudyard Kipling got it just about right, some three centuries later: "I am the Oracle who walks by herself, and all places"—most places—"are alike to me."

Of course, Lady Charlotte wanted to know the same thing. "Mirror," she demanded, her imperious alto as enervating as ever, "are you a divine messenger sent from the Heavens?"

"I am the Oracle," I replied.

"What is your creed?"

"To do no harm."

"Several of my retainers have been injured. Two have been killed. If this accursed siege continues, more will come to grief—possibly including my own person. Yet you do nothing, and this, this *passivité*, it causes harm, even if you think it does not."

I said nothing. This was a tactic, yes, a strategy designed to make her uncomfortable, but also, I could not think of what to say. My villa suddenly seemed very big, and very empty. So many rooms, and most of them filled with mirrors. Why did Mother and Gran and her forebears make so many? Was it simply to pass the time? I hoped not, for there I was, with a remote and in fact undiscoverable island paradise all to myself, but when would I ever know peace?

Shutting up Lady Charlotte seemed like a good first step. I had several options, none of them good. One was to stop replying, but that would violate my family's most basic codes and leave me a shambling wreck besides. Another was to disable Lady Charlotte's mirror by breaking its companion, the one in my villa. It's not difficult to do—glass is glass—but the ramifications are…unpredictable. Shatter a normal mirror and you release nothing more than its basic binding energy; shatter a magic mirror and you release the will of its creator, chaos held in check. Hence the old wives' tales about seven years of bad luck. Break the wrong mirror, and that could quite literally be true.

I had a third option. If I could rescue Lathom House sooner rather than later, I might not only do Lady Charlotte a good turn, but I could gain some much-needed sleep at the same time. Two birds with one stone. It was a seductive idea.

Pondering this, I spent the afternoon providing harmless council to at least ten other mirror owners, one in China, one in Iceland, several in Spain (they do love mirrors there) and one, rather improbably, in a Pueblo kiva in what is now called New Mexico. For all my gifts, I have not the faintest idea how that mirror got there.

At midnight, when I was once more roused from sleep by the ice water of Lady Charlotte's tremulous call, I made up my mind. I would dare to change the world.

In retrospect, I recognize, of course, that this was a very stupid idea. Hot-headed. A pre-teen caprice. But remember that I was grieving, whether I knew it or not, and that I was very, very tired. How much evil in the world is done from lack of sleep? Ask Stalin. Ask Caligula. Ask Pol Pot.

"Good evening, idiot mirror," said Lady Charlotte, once I reached my glass. "You know Fairfax is like to starve us out."

Idiot mirror? That did it.

"Lady Charlotte," I intoned, "the only idiot here is you."

There was a long pause, then a low laugh, rather unpleasant. "Oh, mirror," said Lady Charlotte, "I think I would get better advice from a ten-year-old scullery maid."

I was all set to deliver an arch, stinging reply, when Lady Charlotte spoke again. "In fact, I do some days wonder," she said, newly sly, "if I am not in fact addressing a ten-year-old. You can talk, yes, but so can a bird, if properly trained."

"And I," I replied, startling even myself, "have heard of a noble or two capable of actual independent thought. Although I confess, I have never met such luminaries myself."

For a moment, my mirror was silent, and then Lady Charlotte let fly with a full-bodied whoop of a laugh.

This, then, was my moment, while her guard was down. I squeezed my eyes shut, grasped the mirror with both hands, and willed myself through.

The world made a soft popping sound, and next thing I knew, I was inside Lady Charlotte Stanley. Inside of her mind, to be precise, and very much in charge of it, though her eyes—my eyes, now—flew wide in surprise. My body remained where it was, in my villa, sitting upright on a stool and quivering slightly, as if receiving tiny shocks of electricity. The rest of me, the parts that mattered, were now in Lathom House, in Lady Charlotte's busily wallpapered boudoir, where she had just been in the act of removing a pair of enormous emerald earrings.

And yes, this is how I came to discover that Lady Charlotte was a rather large woman.

I knew at once that Lady Charlotte had done only a few of the things that I, as mirror and Oracle, had insisted she do. She had received Fairfax's emissaries, yes, even going to so far as to host Fairfax himself for a week, but once the siege had begun in earnest, with ordnance flinging cannonballs at Lathom's walls, she had retreated to her chambers and made no showing at all to her captains. In fact, if the gossip of Lady Charlotte's mind was to be believed—and I had access to all of it, if I wanted, though I mostly did not—then her entire household was ready to capitulate at a moment's notice, and would have been quite happy to barter her to the Roundheads in return for their safety.

I was not surprised. One need not be an oracle to make reasonable predictions.

My course, however, was clear, and I began by pulling the cord to summon Lady Charlotte's chambermaid. Jane, her name was, and clearly nervous to be summoned back to her ladyship's presence so soon after bidding her good night.

"Yes'm?" she said, dropping a curtsy.

"*Mon épée*," I said. "*Apportez-le moi.*"

She blinked, surprised, and I must have looked somewhat pop-eyed myself. I had not meant to address her in French, however clumsy, but somehow the interweaving of my mind with Lady Charlotte's had left French as the quickest passage between mind and tongue. With an effort, I tried again.

"My sword," I said. "Bring me my sword, at once."

This time, as I said it, I realized through Lady Charlotte's recollections that I—she—owned no such thing. She'd never so much as touched a sword. This was going to be harder than I thought.

Before Jane could say, "What sword, your ladyship?" which I could see was on the tip of her perplexed tongue, I said, "Get me any sword with heft that you can find. Also, get me a mail shirt, a light helm, and some decent boots. Breeches, if you have any that will fit. I am going out."

"Out?" repeated Jane. "Out where?"

I waved in the direction of the window. "I go to face the enemy," I said, "and you will announce this to everyone you meet. Now hurry. We have little time."

Jane fairly flew from the room, and I settled in to get a better grip on Lady Charlotte's increasingly terrified emotions. She had a great many objections to my plan, but I subdued her in the end. Lucky me, of all the facets of Mother's training, it was projection at which I most excelled. "Because you are willful," Mother had said, smiling in a way that suggested more worry than delight. "Be cautious, or it will be your undoing."

Not an hour later, a bevy of armor-ignorant maids had me dressed more or less like a soldier, and I took to the inner battlements to address my surprised, recently roused troops. It was nearing midnight, with a half moon skimming over patches of sleepy cloud, and I was painfully aware that the entire courtyard smelled of horse piss and fear. Still, this was my moment. Lady Charlotte's moment. It was time to turn the tide.

"My friends," I began, trying for a clarion, booming voice, which Lady Charlotte simply did not possess, "I grow tired of waiting. I grow tired of being some patient hunter's prey. Tonight, by your leave, we shall be prey no longer, but shall, rather, live up to the House of Stanley and to noble Lancashire itself. We suffer invaders from without, invaders who this very night have had the temerity to fire shot, stones, and garbage at our walls. But these walls are our house, are they not? And even in the absence of his Lordship the Earl, do we not have a duty to defend our names, our home, and our honor? I say we do. And I say we prove it this very hour."

If in hindsight all this seems repetitive and bombastic, bear in mind that Lady Charlotte's retainers had never heard her speak thus, so I think I may be forgiven for belaboring my point. To their credit, the good folk of Lathom House liked the idea of sudden action, a bold attack. To a man, I could see my garrison would prefer almost anything to simply sitting around and waiting. All they had lacked was a leader, and inspiration. I, a twelve-year-old who wasn't even physically there, had just provided both.

A muted cheer went up from my men, muted because I quickly shushed them. Enthusiasm we needed, yes, but we needed also the element of surprise.

"To the gates!" I cried. "And follow me, all whose hearts are stout and true!"

It took some time to muster ourselves—lowering a chained drawbridge takes absurdly long—but within the hour, we were on our way, two hundred men on foot, forty on horseback, and the rest remaining behind to man our towers' cannon. These commenced firing just as soon as we crossed the moat, and I don't doubt that Fairfax's men must have thought that we were out of our minds.

Lady Charlotte certainly was. She (and I) sallied forth on horseback, both for its symbolic value and because it seemed the only realistic option. The simple act of trudging up and down Lathom's various staircases had winded me, which was a very odd sensation. I was a limber girl, used to climbing trees, scaling cliffs, and swimming in the sea. To be suddenly lodged in a forty-five-year-old's body, and a puffy, ill-kept one to boot, was a definite shock. Had I led the attack on foot, with the added weight of a mail shirt, a helm, and a broadsword, I doubt I would have made it fifty yards. Even staying atop my horse took a concerted effort. Still, I had a part to play, and I played it to the hilt.

"Charge!" I roared (though Lady Charlotte's cultured voice was certainly unsuited to roaring). And charge we did, with our cannons booming overhead and balls thundering into the enemy positions with *thwumps* of earth-hurling impact.

I had no intention of conquering Fairfax, or even mounting a frontal assault. What I wanted was to disable as much of his artillery as possible, to get back with a minimum of fuss, and give Lady Charlotte's people something to cheer about. All of which sounded good. In the abstract.

First, on the way up and over our outer embankments, I was thrown from my horse, which did more than wind me, it broke my wrist. Or, rather, Lady Charlotte's. Then, once I'd been helped back into the saddle, I discovered that all but two of my excitable soldiers had hurried on without me.

I decided I'd better make an impression, so I drew my sword and began whirling it over my head and yelling at the top of my lungs in French. Sadly, Lady Charlotte was not strong-armed, and the treacherous sword somehow slithered from my grasp (it landed in the mud) just as I arrived at the first of Fairfax's ordnance. This did not matter much, as the Roundheads guarding these cannon had already been killed or made prisoner by the first wave of my men, and my sword was quietly handed back to me by a young officer who seemed quite amazed that I even knew to grasp the pommel and not the blade.

"Onward!" I cried, turning my horse along the flanks of the enemy's line. "Fifty pounds to the first man who reaches the next cannon!"

This spurred everyone in earshot, which was unfortunate, since we all wound up galloping away from our first target without properly disabling the cannon we'd started with. What can I say? In the heat of the moment, I was not the mature Oracle my mother would have been. Indeed, I was excited beyond anything I'd ever experienced before.

From Fairfax's camp came the firing of arquebuses, and I heard swords clashing in all directions. Torches flared like wavering fireflies. A cannonball—one of ours, I believe—fell quite close to me and shied my horse so that I nearly fell again, but with a miraculous piece of equestrian skill, I managed to keep in my saddle, impressing even Lady Charlotte. "*Stupéfier!*" she exclaimed, from somewhere deep inside herself. "I ride like a Hun at *le cirque!*"

At the next clutch of cannon, I arrived in time to raise my sword against an actual enemy soldier. He probably would have killed me, but he stopped his blade mid-swing when he realized he was about to disembowel a lady. I returned the favor by conking him on the head with the flat of my blade, and he very obligingly dropped like felled timber.

On my orders, my men made certain that this new set of cannons would not fire again, or at least not without significant repairs, and then I ordered the retreat. I could see the Roundhead encampment massing for a counter-attack, and while it was tempting to take them on, I knew that would serve no one's purpose, not even theirs.

"Fall back!" I cried. "In the name of Lord James Stanley, Lathom House, and Lancashire, fall back!"

Oh, but I was tired by the time our horses clattered into Lathom's cobbled courtyard; the whole castle rang with the sound of our triumphant hoofbeats. But tired is perhaps not the word. Exhausted beyond all measure, that would be closer to the mark. I tried to induce Lady Charlotte to give a second speech, a cry of defiance that would echo through Lathom House for the duration of the siege, but I could not rouse the woman. In place of oratory, she and her throbbing, swollen wrist were bundled upstairs to her chamber, where her maids peeled off her armor and most of her clothes and laid her flat on her back on the silks of her too-soft bed.

"*Je meurs*," said Lady Charlotte, her voice faint. "I shall be dead by morning."

"I doubt it," I said, possibly aloud. "One thing is certain. When you next show your face, your people will look at you very differently."

Lady Charlotte drifted off to sleep, and I let her go. Then I let myself go, back to my body, my island, and my side of the linked mirrors. I felt just as wrung out as Lady Charlotte, and I slid off my stool to collapse on the floorboards, spent.

Lady Charlotte did not invoke the privileges of her mirror for five days after that night, and when she did, it was with a new and very welcome timidity. Better still, broken wrist and all, she was thankful. My midnight sortie had done the trick. Her retainers were now one hundred percent loyal, ready to die before they'd even speak the word surrender. Indeed, they'd mounted a second raid (just as the Oracle had said they should) and it had gone almost as well as the first. As for Fairfax, he'd begun offering all sorts of attractive terms, but to each of these, Lady Charlotte had offered very haughty versions of "Fiddlesticks!"

Even so, she had a question. "Must it still be June?" she asked. "It is a long time to wait. Even our barley flour runs short."

I had already peered into time's new course—as both my buckets and my heaving stomach could attest—and I told Lady Charlotte, quite confidently, that Prince Rupert would arrive in the last week of May, a month earlier than time had previously planned, in part because of the good reports he was now hearing about Lathom's courageous defenders.

"*Mai*," mused Lady Charlotte, sounding not displeased. "I believe we can last though May."

"You can," I said. "The Oracle of the mirror has spoken."

I had meant to end the conversation there, but Lady Charlotte had more on her mind. "You say you are an Oracle," she ventured, choosing her words with care, "but I have felt you, when you—how shall I say? Visited me. You are an Oracle, and powerful, yes. But my guess was right. You are also a child. Do you have a mother? Someone to look after you?"

That tripped me. It had been weeks, after all, since Mother had died, and what with feeding myself, taking care of the villa, and managing the mirrors, I had hardly had time to think of her—of her absence, and my loss. But in that moment, with those simple words from a faraway woman whom I did not much care for, I was stripped of all my defenses. I began quaking like a poplar in a stiff wind.

"I am the Oracle," I said, as best I could. "I do not need care."

"All of us need care," said Lady Charlotte. Then she rushed on, as if certain she would lose her nerve. "I know you do not like me, and I know also that you would prefer that I leave you alone. But I would ask that you grant this much to a grateful woman who owes you more than she can ever repay. Allow me, now and then, to look in on you. With my mirror. To say '*Bonjour, et comment allez-vous?*'"

I could not answer, though I tried. A mighty sob, unstoppable, had hold of my throat. But Lady Charlotte was patient, and she stayed with me until I was calmer, and able to speak.

"I know what it is to have children," she said, so softly that I could barely hear. "And I remember, too, believe it or not, what it is like to *be* a child. And just as children are a blessing, we must take time to bless the children, so. To my *petit oracle, Dieu bénissez-vous.*"

That night, I slept better than I had in a month, and when I awoke, it was my birthday. Overnight, I had turned thirteen. I went outside, practiced my birdcalls, and went to the place where I had cremated Mother's body. I sang her a song, and hoped she could hear me, and when I was done, I went back to my villa, this house of many mirrors, ready at last to be the Oracle that I still am today, and feeling for the first time that I had some hope of living up to my difficult, wonderful task.

Mark Rigney has had over fifty short pieces find print in a gentle arc covering the last two decades, with stories in Lightspeed, Realms of Fantasy, and more. Theatrical credits, too, with play across the U.S., including off-Broadway, along with Canada, Hong Kong, Nepal, and Australia.

Watchlist

Mark Bilsborough

Again, way too much fine film and TV to go through. Not so much film, because Hollywood's still semi-sitting on its hands, but new super-expensive TV abounds, and it would be remiss of me not to point you in the right direction.

First off, there's an epic battle going on in the word of fantasy TV, as the defining work of the genre, *Lord of the Rings*, gets a prequel airing in the $500 (rumoured) first season of **Rings of Power**, up against (um, 'coincidentally') the *Game of Throne's* prequel **House of the Dragon.** Of course we're all still smarting over the botched ending of the original *Game of Thrones* series so we approached this with weary trepidation but so far, half a season on, this completely blows the overstuffed *Rings of Power* out of the water.

And that's not just because the *Rings of Power* people apparently have no idea (or dust don't care) what *Lord of the Rings* (the book) was all about. You could lay that charge at the films, too, but at least they didn't drag so and trip themselves over with unnecessary CGI and limp characterization). And *Rings of Power* doesn't have Matt Smith and his flowing blonde locks, which House of the Dragon does to great effect. *House* is all about House Targaryen (the mad ones) and it seems to be leading up to full on bonkers-ness. Hands down winner. Sorry, Amazon – money doesn't always win.

Second, **The Sandman** – Neil Gaiman's epic comic adaptation (admittedly of his own comic) now streaming on Netflix. Gaiman's translation to screen has been patchy, The films *Stardust* and *Coraline* are both excellent but on the small screen, *Neverwhere* and *American Gods* (and to a certain extent *Good Omens*) have been disappointing shadows of their book incarnations. Even Gaiman's *Doctor Who* episodes have underwhelmed. *Sandman*, on the other hand, is well worth watching. Lord Morpheous, necromancy, death and dreams – plus demons, inventiveness and moody settings.

Thirdly, *The Man who Fell to Earth* on Paramount/Showtime is worth a look. It's a sequel rather than a remake of the 1976 movie with David Bowie in the title role, and this time Bill Nighy plays Thomas Jerome Newton. The plot follows the arrival of another alien visitor (Faraday – played by Chiwetel Eijofor), summoned by Newton to help save his species. And, like the original, it's more an exploration of humanity than a depiction of aliens. It's pacy and atmospheric, with some of the weirdness that made the movie stand out. Making it a reverential, direct sequel is a great strength and the impressive cast (including Naomi Harris) do it justice. Second series, please.

A brief mention for *She-Hulk: Attorney at Law,* which critics love and the audience, seemingly, doesn't. Except that the show's been repeatedly review-bombed by people who should know better, artificially lowering the score. Strong female lead, female writing team, scripts poking fun at male self-importance? Well we love it. It's funny, sharply written, different and has the outstanding Tatiana Maslany (*Orphan Black*) in the title role, turning green when she gets an accidental blood transfusion from her cousin Bruce (aka The Hulk) then forging a lawyer's life representing super-people such as the Abomination. Loads of cameos and guest slots culminated in the long awaited return of Daredevil, albeit in a silly yellow suit and smiling a bit more than we're used to. We'll have more to say about She-Hulk and Daredevil in the future, but for now check it out on Disney+ and make your own mind up.

Plenty more to watch. No space here for *The Witcher, The Peripheral. Doom Patrol, The Imperfects, Westworld, Tales of the Walking Dead, Andor* or *the Mandalorian,* but they're all worth watching.

I'm going to close this column, though, with a brief look at *Prey,* the latest in the Predator series and the first to go out exclusively on streaming services (a mistake: this film has Big Screen written all over it). It uses the same old format – group of people out in the wild tracked down one by one by a merciless alien hunter with stealth tech and a blood lust – but the twist is that this is set in 1719, in the US Great Plains and the hero is a Comanche woman warrior. Top-notch filmmaking and easily the best Predator film to date.

Bookworm

Sandra Baker and Mark Bilsborough

Chivalry

*By Neil Gaiman &
Colleen Doran*

Chivalry was first published by Neil Gaiman in his 1998 collection of short fiction: *'Smoke and Mirrors'*. It's the story of an elderly widow who buys what turns out to be the Holy Grail in a charity shop. An amusing and often poignant adventure ensues, as Galaad, an earnest medieval knight comes to claim the cup.

Now released as a graphic novel, *'Chivalry'* glitters and glows with the impeccable illustrations of Colleen Doran, who also worked with Gaiman on *Snow, Glass, Apples*.

I say 'glitters' because Doran originally envisaged her work as an actual illuminated manuscript with gold leaf and iridescent colours. These techniques proved unworkable in production terms, but you still get a feel for the majesty and grandeur of her original ideas.

It also comes across as a work of love – Doran waited many many years before having the opportunity to turn *Chivalry* into a graphic novel. Her depiction of the main characters – Mrs Whitaker and Galaad – are tender and mellow. The attentions to detail are clearly carefully researched, right down to the ubiquitous tea set because of course, the first thing Mrs Whitaker does when

Galaad comes to claim the Grail is to offer him a cup of tea.

There are some wonderful moments, where Doran interprets Gaiman's prose with a single illustration – I particularly liked the 'not bothered' shrugs of Marie the charity shop assistant and then her 'makeover' after she has met and fallen for Galaad.

Chivalry is a story of realising what is important in life. It makes us consider what we truly treasure and what is the meaning of treasure – is it a memory, a good life, or is it something we want to possess? The contrast between the magical Arthurian quest for the Holy Grail is contrasted delightfully and thoughtfully with the ordinariness of the day-to-day life of a lonely widow who misses her late husband.

It's a short read, but I found myself re-reading it and reverently stroking the pages as I went along. It's a book that feels like a gift and there are fifteen pages at the end devoted (somewhat indulgently) to a commentary from Doran about the making of the book and several of her original sketches. I had not read the original short story, so each page was a revelation. I'm not sure if I would have been quite so enamoured if it was a story I was already familiar with, but it certainly looks great on the bookshelf.

Tick Tock

By Simon Mayo

Yes, *the* Simon Mayo. The radio presenter. So this is another of those books written by people you've heard of in another life. I think he's a good radio presenter. He was a good DJ back on Radio 1 (I'm old, I know) and his film review podcast with Mark Kermode is most entertaining. But a *writer*? I'm assuming he didn't have the same kind of hassle the rest of us face in getting a publishing deal, but you never know. So the cynic in me opened the pages of *Tick Tock* warily, but hey, for all their limitations I enjoyed Richard Osman's runaway bestsellers, so maybe media personalities can be the next Booker winners.

Tick Tock's not going to win the Booker. Or the Hugo's. But it's considerably more entertaining than I'd expected, and I'm happy to give it a cautious thumbs up.

The plot doesn't break much new ground and I think it's too early for a novel like this, but this kicks off as a pandemic story about a new disease in its early stages. It veers off into espionage thriller before the bodies start to pile up, but the gist is that kids in a London school start to get a ticking in their ears, which leads to deafness, which leads to death. Soon there are outbreaks throughout London and elsewhere, including a cluster in Salisbury, where much of the action takes place (expect a connection with real events). The story follows Kit, Head of English, and his daughter Rose, plus his girlfriend Lilly, who helpfully turns out to be a virologist. Rose's friend starts ticking and so Rose sets up a WhatsApp group to gather stories, starts a school closure protest, is blamed for a hospital riot and attracts the interest of the press. Lilly's estranged father has just died too, but there's something odd about the mourners in the crematorium. Jess, Rose and Kit flee to Salisbury (where all plot threads lead) to find answers. Various Government

agencies start to show an interest, and they're not all benign.

All tenuously sci-fi, of course, but it is an extrapolation of current trends and past events so it just about slips under the wire, though I suspect Mayo and his publishers would describe it as a thriller (and I doubt you'll find it on the sci-fi shelves). Grounding it in London school makes it more prosaic than I'd like, and the tight character focus means the wider pandemic story never gets a chance to properly develop. It's a slow burn too, but it's an easy read and I didn't see the twist coming, which always suggests good writing to me. Some of the cover quotes are hyperbolic, so I'd advise ignoring them (you really can't '*feel the tension and fear in every page*') but it's competent enough. And entertaining.

The Extracted Trilogy

By RR Haywood (audiobook narrated by Carl Prekopp)

I'm not normally one for audio books, but I do like a good listen on a long car journey. Which is how I discovered the 'Extracted' trilogy. It's been my motorway companion for many miles and, I have to confess, on the 40-degree heat red alert day in the UK, I lay on the sofa and listened to it for hours. It's all I had the energy to do; don't judge!

Anyway, the premise of the trilogy is how a group of three dead heroes travel through time to save the world. Dead? Yes, originally, but they are all 'extracted' from the moment before their individual deaths to form a team

that will jump around in time to prevent the end of civilisation in 2111.

So, we have Ben Ryder – an insurance investigator who single handedly prevented a terrorist attack on London in the 1980s; Safa Patel, an elite police officer who died saving the British Prime Minister; and Harry Madden, a legendary World War Two hero. In charge of them is Roland, whose gifted son Bertie invents a time machine in 2061 to prevent his father committing suicide. It is Bertie's travels to the different timelines that reveal the end of the world in 2111.

To train for their mission and to escape detection, the extracted heroes are based in a homemade bunker on a hillside in the Cretaceous period, complete with dinosaurs roaming the plains beneath them.

Book 1, 'Extracted' is followed by 'Executed' and 'Extinct'. Each book is an action focused, very visual and often very funny journey to save the world. What puts this trilogy above any other similar time twisting novels you may have read is the quality and depth of the characters and the way they interact with each other. There is plenty of humour and banter between Safa, Ben and Harry. The dialogue is natural and sharp and no-one takes themselves too seriously.

In the audible version, the narrator – Carl Prekopp – makes full use of the writer's flair for characterisation. A simple 'aye' from Harry Madden (he's from Yorkshire) often makes a whole scene memorable. Prekopp is good with accents and his timing matches Haywood's pace perfectly.

In 2018, the Extracted trilogy was optioned for a TV series. I can see it working really well – lots of plot twists and plenty of cinematic set pieces: from destructive dinosaur attacks to mind-blowing WW2 air raids in Berlin to laser drone strikes in 22nd century London.

A tv series would also remove what is my only real criticism for these books – the over explanatory tone of the writing, particularly in the first book. Often, the action is detailed too closely, conversations are too lengthy and Haywood can often take ages to describe a five minute moment. If I'd been reading the paper or kindle version of these books, I must confess that there would have been a number of times that I would have skipped through certain passages.

It's definitely worth persevering with the trilogy though. The writing does improve and the characters will not let you go without a fight. Recommended.